Circles in the Snow

Circles in the Snow

A Bo Tully Mystery

by
Patrick F. McManus

Skyhorse Publishing

Copyright © 2014 by Patrick F. McManus

All Rights Reserved. No part of this book may be reproduced in any manner without the express written consent of the publisher, except in the case of brief excerpts in critical reviews or articles. All inquiries should be addressed to Skyhorse Publishing, 307 West 36th Street, 11th Floor, New York, NY 10018.

Skyhorse Publishing books may be purchased in bulk at special discounts for sales promotion, corporate gifts, fund-raising, or educational purposes. Special editions can also be created to specifications. For details, contact the Special Sales Department, Skyhorse Publishing, 307 West 36th Street, 11th Floor, New York, NY 10018 or info@skyhorsepublishing.com.

Skyhorse® and Skyhorse Publishing® are registered trademarks of Skyhorse Publishing, Inc.®, a Delaware corporation.

www.skyhorsepublishing.com

10 9 8 7 6 5 4 3 2 1

Library of Congress Cataloging-in-Publication Data is available on file.

ISBN: 978-1-62914-170-1

Printed in the United States of America

Dedication

To my beautiful wife, Darlene "Bun" McManus,
without whose extensive labors and keen eye for
detail this novel never would have been completed.

Acknowledgments

The author of *Circles in the Snow* wishes to thank Matt Kelso for sharing with him his knowledge of archery and bow hunting.

Chapter 1

Blight County Sheriff Bo Tully stood on snowshoes atop a knoll overlooking the Blight River. It was only the second week of December, and already the snow was nearly three feet deep. Tully stood six feet two inches and was a bit stout, appearing even more so in his faded red mackinaw and bulky black wool pants. A tiny icicle hung from the droopy tip of his thick, graying mustache. He peered at the dark forest across the river. The trees were filled with eagles, newly arrived from California to feed on the run of kokanee salmon in the lake and river. The eagles' dark feathers made them almost invisible against the background of the forest, but the topknots of their heads glowed like hundreds of white Christmas tree ornaments. He turned and yelled at a skinny old man, also on snowshoes. "Pap, get over here! I got something for you to see. You can be witness to the fact I haven't gone crazy in my old age!"

Pap waddled over in the peculiar gait of a man attached to a pair of bear-paw snowshoes. He wore a red plaid wool cap with loose earflaps, a red mackinaw, and laced leather boots halfway to his knees. His pant legs were tucked into the boots. "Whatcha find, Bo? I ain't got much reputation as a witness."

Pap Tully was the smartest man Tully knew, but he put on a pretense of being a normal resident of Blight County, where ignorance was prized as a virtue. A Blight County person who read anything except out of necessity was suspect and probably dangerous. Pap was approaching eighty now, an age when one is unlikely to be found traipsing about the mountains on snowshoes. But Tully was sure the old man could still raise the average IQ in any Blight County room merely by walking into it—the more crowded the room, the better. Pap was Tully's father.

Pap had been one of a long line of corrupt and deadly Blight County sheriffs. His son, Bo Tully, had been the first sheriff to break the mold, with a career in office marked by honesty, integrity, ingenuity, and effectiveness, not to mention sending most of the county's resident criminal life off to prison at one time or another. His father, Pap, now one of the wealthiest residents of the county, viewed him as the black sheep of the family, a man destined for relative poverty amid the riches of the state, all of which could be easy pickings for a sheriff adequately bright and sufficiently corrupt. It was enough to make a father sick to his stomach.

Pap and Bo had been out doing a survey of grouse killed by an unknown predator, a project they had taken on as a service to the Idaho Department of Fish and Game. "I just found another pile of grouse feathers next to a tree," Pap said, coming up beside Tully. "I don't reckon it was killed there and eaten raw by a human."

"I hope not," Tully said. "If so, I don't want to meet the human, although several possible suspects come to mind. Now look down there, Pap, at that island in the middle of the river."

The old man pulled down the bill of his cap and squinted at the island. It was covered with snow, the top layer fresh, probably having fallen in the last few days. In it he could see the clear outline of a large circle. "Weird," he said. "No doubt the work of some kids."

Tully nodded. "That's what I thought at first. But notice, there are no tracks going to or coming from the circle. Also, anyone making it would have had to wade out to the island or try to land a boat on it, a maneuver in those swift currents and shallow water on both sides that would make a landing mighty tricky. Also, the circle is perfectly round, as if drawn in the snow with a giant protractor. Can you make out that dark spot right in the middle, where the point of the protractor must have been stuck?"

"Yeah! Kind of spooky, ain't it? Had to have been done by somebody hanging over it, maybe from a helicopter."

"Couldn't be a helicopter," Tully said. "That would have blown all the snow off the island."

"Makes it even more spooky. That circle must be over six feet across. Maybe it was made by one of them flying saucers. I read somewhere they're suspected of making circles in wheat fields."

"Good point. I wouldn't write off flying saucers myself. I saw one once, you know."

Pap gave his son an uneasy glance. "I didn't know that."

"Yeah, I did. I was seventeen years old and working on that crew constructing a power line over the Cabinet Mountains. There had been quite a few saucer sightings reported around the country that summer, so I had been hoping I might see one. Because I was the youngest and most useless member of the crew, the foreman sent me back to our previous site to pick up a tool that had been left behind. When I returned with the tool, coming up around a steep curve on the mountain, I saw a huge saucer hanging almost over the crew, no higher than the tops of the fir trees nearby. It was the most beautiful thing I've ever seen, glowing all silvery and perfectly still. It was huge, and its occupants were obviously interested in what our crew was up to. But all of the men were down on their knees bolting together the steel leg of a tower. Not one of them would look up. I couldn't believe they weren't astounded by the sight. I blurted out, 'What is that thing, anyway?' One guy down on the far end of the leg, without looking up, said, 'It's a weather balloon.' Well, I knew it wasn't a weather balloon, but I didn't want to be fired for standing around gawking at the thing, so I dropped down and started poking bolts in holes. When I looked up again, it was gone, vanished without a sound. No one on the crew ever mentioned it. I guess some folks just don't like to see things they don't believe in."

"That's right," Pap said. "I'm one of them."

"Well, you've seen this circle, and I need a witness to the fact, someone who can testify I'm not going crazy."

"What circle is that, Bo?"

Tully shook his head. "Let's get back to our grouse survey. How many signs of dead grouse have we found so far?"

Pap pulled a twisted wad of paper out of his pants pocket and checked it. "The last sign I spotted came to nine for this knoll alone. The predator keeps up this pace there won't be no grouse left at all. You think maybe the eagles are killing and eating them?"

Tully thought about this. "Naw, eagles are too big. They would crash and burn, flying into a tree to pick off a grouse. Has to be something smaller, maybe a chicken hawk."

"That's a red-tailed hawk," Pap said. "But they're small enough to zoom into a tree and pick off a grouse."

"Yeah," Tully said. "A red-tail seems about right. On the other hand, I'd rather keep a hawk around than a grouse any day. A grouse isn't much of a step up from a chicken when it comes to intelligence. A hawk is practically a genius compared to a grouse." He turned from the river and started tramping across the clearing behind him. Suddenly he stopped, noticing a flutter in the snow near the wood line. "Some feathers over there, Pap."

"Yeah, I just saw them myself. What the devil! I think that's the tip of an arrow sticking out of the snow!"

They plodded over to the object. "It's an arrow, all right," Tully said. He squatted down on his snowshoes and tugged on the tip of the shaft. The arrow didn't budge. "Must be stuck in a log. Step off your snowshoes, Pap, and use one of them to shovel out what it's stuck to."

Imitating a child's voice, Pap said, "I don't wanna, Bo."

Tully glared at him. "Oh, all right, I'll do it myself. Should've known better than to go out snowshoeing with a sissy."

He unfastened his snowshoes and stepped off, sinking into the snow halfway up to his hips. The grainy snow pushed up the legs of his long underwear and rasped against his skin. He bent down and used one of his snowshoes to fling away large scoops of snow.

Pap looked down on him as he worked. "Don't know how somebody could shoot an arrow into a log and have it stand straight up like that."

Tully stopped shoveling. "Good point, Pap. Maybe I should wait until I get one of the deputies up here. They enjoy all this grisly stuff." He began scooping the snow back with tiny motions. After a bit he stopped and looked up at the old man. "What we have here is a body, shot through the back with an arrow. I've investigated a few murders in my time, but this is the first to employ an arrow." He used the snowshoe to shovel out a space so he could squat down next to the body.

Pap looked down from his perch atop the snowshoes. "Could be an accident."

Tully shook his head. "Bow hunters don't do accidents. Rifle hunters are known to, but not bow hunters. When a hunter draws an arrow on something, he knows precisely what he's aiming at. It's a whole lot different from some idiot snapping off a quick shot with a rifle. We'd better get the medical examiner up here pronto." He stood up and pulled out his cell phone. "We have a murder on our hands."

Pap's shoulders sagged. "Tell Susan to bring along a carrier that scoots along on the surface of the snow. And for her crew to wear snowshoes, because I ain't helpin' with this job."

Tully frowned and spoke into the phone. "This is the sheriff, Ginny. Get me Susan, please."

"One second, Bo. She's out in the back room doing some stuff."

"Doing some stiff?" Tully said.

"No, Sheriff, not stiff! Stuff!"

"Oh, sorry. I never know what might be going on in that morgue of yours." He winked at Pap, who grinned back.

The medical examiner picked up. "What is it this time, Bo?"

"Looks like we've got a murder up here along the river, Susan. At least murder is my guess right now. I'll await your expert opinion. The body has an arrow going right through between the shoulder blades and probably all the way to the back of the breastplate. Doesn't strike me as a suicide."

"An arrow! Anybody you know?"

"Haven't seen the face and don't plan on doing so until you get up here. We're on the South River Road about a mile past Trapper Creek. You'll see my Explorer parked off to the side."

"Gotcha, Bo. Should be there with my crew in about an hour. See you then."

"The snow is deep here, Susan, so you'd better come prepared with snowshoes and a toboggan or something you can use to haul the body out over the snow."

"We'll come prepared. Don't mess with the body."

"There you go again, spoiling the little fun I get."

Chapter 2

Tully heard the sound of a vehicle pulling up and stopping. He turned and looked. It wasn't one of the ME's. It was a battered old black pickup truck with SILVER TIP MINER printed on the door of the cab in big white letters. A pudgy little man got out, threw down a pair of cross-country skis, and began gliding directly toward Tully. It was August Finn, the editor and only reporter for the *Silver Tip Miner* weekly newspaper. Augie was a major thorn in Tully's psyche. One of the people in the medical examiner's office must have tipped him off. Tully estimated that Augie had hundreds of tipsters scattered around the county. They no doubt were the reason he was able single-handedly to fill his newspaper each week. Tully actually enjoyed the paper, except when it featured him.

Augie glided up on his skis. Tully glared at him. "Who was it?"

Augie gave him his surprised look. "Who, Bo?"

"You know who. Who in the ME's office tipped you we have a murder out here?"

"A murder! What a stroke of luck! I just happened to be passing by and saw your rig parked alongside the road. Is that the body half-buried down there in the snow?"

Tully's shoulders sagged in surrender. "Yes, Augie, that's the body. Don't take another step closer to it. Otherwise, I will have to shoot you for disturbing a crime scene, not to mention I would simply enjoy it. So put that camera away."

The reporter laughed and slid the camera back inside his jacket. "I see you've got your father looking after you, Sheriff. How you doing, Pap?"

"Great, Augie! Nothing I like better than a good murder."

"Me neither. Okay, Bo, I'll wait until the ME gets here and takes over. She's much more flexible."

"It was Susan who tipped you to the murder, wasn't it?"

"Susan who, Bo?"

The medical examiner's white Suburban, emergency lights flashing, pulled up and stopped on the road. A black hearse pulled in behind it. Tully, Pap, and Augie stood next to the pile of snow by the hole, all three hunched over with their hands in their pockets. With great difficulty, Tully had managed to climb out of the hole and get his snowshoes back on. Three attendants and Susan got out of the van and strapped on snowshoes, the modern kind with aluminum frames and pink plastic in place of webbing. Neither Tully, Pap, nor Augie would have been caught dead wearing such contraptions, although they knew the modern devices were lighter and more maneuverable than what they were wearing, snowshoes of bent hickory frames and leather webbing, probably used by the first mountain men to hike over the Rockies. They were partially held together with bailing wire, not that there was anything wrong with that.

Susan and her assistants, Hap Rogers, Glenn Duncan, and Willy Sims, plodded over, none of them displaying any indication they had ever worn snowshoes before. Two of the assistants carried shovels and one pulled a long aluminum half shell apparently intended for hauling the body back to the hearse, the driver of which leaned against his vehicle smoking a cigarette as he watched the proceedings from a distance.

Susan stopped at the edge of the hole. With the snow Tully had flung out around its edges, it was now over four feet deep. She gazed down into it, a wisp of her blond hair drifting in the breeze. She pursed her lips. "This is my first arrow shooting."

"Mine, too," Tully said, glancing at Susan. She was extraordinarily pretty, particularly for a medical examiner. He wouldn't mind renewing his affair with her. So many women, so little time. Susan smiled at Augie. "As usual, I see the *Silver Tip Miner* is one of the first at the scene. How are you, Augie?"

"Great, Susan. I just happened to be passing by when I saw Bo's rig parked out on the road."

Tully frowned. "You use this road often to get to town?"

"Oh yeah, Bo, maybe every other day. It does away with some of the monotony of driving the same old highway between Silver Tip and Blight City day after day."

Tully nodded. "So you don't mind that the South River Road is across the river from Silver Tip and you have to drive twenty extra miles just to hit the bridges."

Susan smiled, then said, "Glenn, you and Willy drop down in the hole and shovel the snow away on one side of the body, wide enough so we can get the shell in there next to it. Then I'll send Hap down. He can take the feet. Glenn and Will, each of you take a shoulder, and the three of you lift it straight up and lay it face down in the tub. Keep it as flat and straight as you can. I'm sure it's frozen solid, so that shouldn't be a problem. Don't mess with the arrow."

"We weren't about to," Glenn said. He and Willy took off their snowshoes and slid into the hole.

Interesting, Tully thought, *the dead man has already become an "it."*

A large crow flew over and landed on a treetop in the woods next to them. Bobbing back and forth, it began to caw furiously, staring down at the scene. Tully looked up at it and muttered, "Yeah yeah, I know, old fellow, you saw the whole thing go down. Too bad none of us speaks crow."

Apparently disgusted by lack of interest in its report, the crow flew off. Tully stared after it, tugging on the icy corner of his mustache. Birds were such strange creatures. Weird, actually.

A breeze had come up and the chill of it shot through Tully's mackinaw. He thrust his hands into his pockets and shivered as he watched the three young men work. He wished he had worn gloves. Pap had long ago taught him that gloves were for sissies, and he had never felt comfortable wearing them, particularly when Pap was in the vicinity. It now occurred to him that maybe Pap was simply too cheap to buy gloves for the family. He glanced at the old man. Pap was watching the activity in the hole with keen interest. Nothing aroused his father's interest more than a good murder.

Once the snow had been shoveled away, Susan slid the shell down and the three assistants lifted the corpse into it, the arrow sticking straight up. Tully and Pap pulled on ropes fastened to each end of the shell and the three assistants lifted and pushed from the bottom. Soon the aluminum carrier was sliding atop the piled snow.

Tully glanced around, looking for the *Silver Tip* newsman. He found him standing a ways back from the hole, furiously snapping photos. The urge came over him to walk over, rip the camera out of Augie's hands, and stomp it into the snow. It would have been immensely satisfying, except he would regret the action when he read about it on the front page of the *Silver Tip Miner.*

"I'll remove the arrow when we get back to the lab," Susan told Tully. "I suppose you'll want it for evidence."

He nodded. "Yeah, this has to be a murder. Arrows don't go off accidentally."

"Hey!" Willy yelled from the hole. "He was layin' on a rifle—a scoped rifle!"

"A rifle?" Tully said. "Don't touch it, Willy. As soon as you guys get the body back in one of your rigs, I'll come down and take a look."

"Gotcha, Sheriff."

"You better climb out of there or your boss might leave without you, Willy. Good work! I could use a sharp lad like you on the force."

"No way you get that kid!" Susan snapped. "He's one of the best I've got."

"Oh, all right, Susan, I'll take the rifle. Not much you can do with that. Suppose I can get a look at our dead guy's face?"

"Sure. He's in no hurry. Hap, tilt the tub up a bit, so Bo can get a look."

Hap, grunting, tilted the tub back and held it. Tully squatted down on his snowshoes and grabbed the hair, lifting up the bearded, frost-encrusted face. Both eyes and the mouth were wide open, as if startled by the pain and impact of the arrow. The teeth were tobacco stained. Blood had dribbled around them and frozen in pink streaks. He straightened up.

"Anybody you know, Bo?" Susan asked.

Tully was silent for a moment, as if pondering something. Then he said, "Afraid so. It's Morgan Fester."

"Fester!" Pap said. "I thought he left last month for his ranch in Mexico!"

"I thought so, too," Tully said. "His hands up here never reported him missing." He released the hair and the head thumped back down into the shell.

"Maybe his hands didn't want to spoil their good luck," Pap said. "I never found Morg that pleasant to be around at any time, and I didn't work for him. Hard even to imagine what that was like."

Susan kicked the shell and indicated with a jerk of her thumb for it to be hauled to the hearse. She looked at Tully. "You think he must have been bad to his workers, how about his wife?"

Tully nodded. "Morg was a mean cuss all right, not to speak ill of the dead. But for all his rottenness, I sort of liked the guy. He was the last of his kind—I hope."

Pap nodded. "From time to time, I liked him, too, but not all that often. In fact, he's one of those persons I wouldn't look too hard for his killer, if I were you, Bo."

Tully shook his head. "Sorry, but the law doesn't work that way, Pap, at least not since you retired as sheriff. Now a murder is a murder and the law requires the killer be found and prosecuted, whether he's a good guy or a bad guy."

"Even if the killer is one of the good guys, you go after him, is that right, Bo?"

"Seems a pity, doesn't it? But that's the way the system is supposed to work. I didn't invent it, so don't blame me."

"I wasn't accusing you of a decency, Bo."

"I know. Well, I'd better drive over to the Fester ranch. His hands would be among my first suspects. I'm sure any one of them would have reason to kill him, such as Fester's taking the price of a lost cow out of his pay."

Susan said, "If you boys are done chatting, I think we'll pack up and leave."

"Please do," Tully said. "Pap and I have to get busy on some police work."

Susan tramped back to the road, followed by Augie. The reporter snapped some pictures of her as she climbed into her Suburban. Tully turned to Pap. "You might as well go home. I'll get my crime scene investigations unit out here to see if it can pick up any clues."

"Crime scene investigations unit?" Pap said. "I didn't know you had one of them."

"Yeah, its name is Lurch, sometimes known as Byron Proctor."

"I know Byron."

"Well, he's one of the best CSI units in the business. Our crime scene is pretty messed up, but there's no telling what Lurch might be able to come up with."

Pap got in his pickup truck and prepared to drive off. Tully suddenly remembered that his father was one of the best trackers he had ever known or even heard about. Lawmen in other counties had often called him in to track a runaway prisoner or suspect. Tully yelled, "Stop!"

The old man almost drove off the road. He rolled down his window and glared at Tully, who walked over, stuck his head in the cab, and said, "I just thought of something. I want you to stay here and help my CSI unit."

"Help him how?"

"You are one of the best trackers I know, Pap. I want you to teach the Unit something about tracking."

"I've worked crimes for you before, Bo, but with this new snow, I doubt I'll be able to turn up anything. There was a time, though, when I could work new snow pretty good."

"I know. It won't hurt to try anyway, just to see what you might come up with. I know you haven't got any other pressing engagements, and the Unit can use your help."

"If you put it that way, I'll wait for the Unit. But he better get a move on."

The eagles across the river had remained on their perches during the entire ruckus, their white heads still glowing against the black background of the forest. Apparently, they were interested observers. Tully was surprised they weren't jumpy, because somebody had been shooting eagles. Residents around the mouth of the river had picked up several of their carcasses floating out into Lake Blight. Some of them had saved feathers, passing them around among friends and neighbors, not realizing it was against the law to possess eagle feathers. Apparently, this flock hadn't been the target, or they would have been a lot more nervous. He lowered himself into the hole, pulled out his handkerchief, and picked up the rifle, a scoped .22-caliber Remington lever-action. He set the rifle on the edge of the hole and climbed out. It seemed likely Fester had intended to shoot eagles with it. He carried the rifle over to his Explorer, stowed it in the luggage section, and radioed the station. Florence, the radio operator, answered. "Blight County Sheriff's office."

"Flo, get me Daisy, please." Daisy Quinn was his secretary.

"One minute, Sheriff. She just stepped out of the office. I think she was headed for the ladies' room."

"She knows I don't allow that during office hours. I'm away half a day and the place falls apart."

"I know, Bo. Without you here, it's all fun and games and going to the bathroom. Ah, here comes Daisy now."

Daisy came on. "I understand you've been haranguing Florence about lack of discipline in the office while you're gone. It may be that our nerves suddenly relax their tension in your absence. What's up?"

"What's up, I've got a murder out here on the South River Road, and I need my CSI unit to check it out."

"A murder! I don't believe it. What next! Anyway, Lurch is busy doing a crossword puzzle at his desk. I'll see if he can manage to break away. The victim anyone we know?"

"Morgan Fester."

"Oh, my gosh! I know a lot of people who would like to murder Fester, but none who would actually do it. You have any suspects?"

"A few hundred. No, not really. I'm about to head over to the Fester ranch and talk to his hired hands. If

anyone wanted to kill him, I suspect it might be someone who worked for him. Or maybe his wife."

"Oh, I know his wife, Bo. We go to the same church.
She's a lovely person. Hillory's spending the winter in
Mexico—Cabo San Lucas. She tells me it's a wonder-
ful place."

"You know how she and Fester got along?"

"Okay, I guess. He lets her do whatever she wants,
such as spending winters in Cabo, and he does whatever he wants."

"And that *was*?"

"Right, he doesn't do any of it anymore, does he?
Mostly, he fooled around with his various girlfriends."

"You happen to know the names of any of the
girlfriends?"

"No, but I could probably find out."

"Please do, Daisy. I need all the help I can get on
this one."

"Sure, Bo. I love this sort of thing! Oh, and he spent
a lot of time in Silver Tip. Or so I've heard from Hillory.
It was practically his home away from home, according to her."

"The town or the brothel?"

"The town couldn't keep anybody entertained—a
few dozen houses the miners and their families live in,
a grocery store, a barbershop, three or four taverns, a
grade school, and, of course, the *Silver Tip Miner*. That's
about it."

"Yeah, I guess you're right. The other Silver Tip
pretty much dominates the name. Do you know federal agents stop by the brothel on a regular basis?"

"I didn't know that. There goes more of our tax money."

"No, Daisy, they just show the ladies some photos of gangsters they're trying to get a lead on, see if they might have stopped by Silver Tip, which I guess would indicate the gangsters were on their way to the West Coast. That brothel is famous all over the country, maybe all over the world, and criminal types seem to go out of their way to pass through there. Maybe some noncriminal types, too, but that's just my guess. Anyway, right now I'm practically freezing to death. Before that happens, I'm headed over to Fester's ranch to talk to his cowhands. Tell the Unit on South River Road about a mile past Trapper Creek he'll come to a knoll by the river. He'll see where the snow is all messed up. That's our crime scene. Pap will be waiting for him. I'll see the two of them back here when I'm done at the Fester ranch."

"Oh, one more thing, Boss."

"And that is?"

"I didn't want to tell you, but I will. The General Store up at Pine Flats was robbed last night."

"Just what I needed! Another crime! Anyone hurt?"

"Yeah, but not too bad. It happened just after the store closed at nine o'clock. Clyde Parker said he had just locked the front door when someone came up behind him and hit him on the head. Parker was raving when he called. He said he didn't see who hit him but that Milo Burk and two other young guys had been lurking around in the back of the store earlier. Milo's two friends left, but Clyde thinks Milo hid somewhere in back until the store closed. He thinks Milo hit him from behind with something and then opened the door for the other two. They cleaned out the cash register and took a couple cases of beer, maybe some other stuff, but Clyde said he doesn't know what. When Clyde came to, the robbers were gone. He didn't report the robbery until this morning, after he'd had a chance to see what the thieves got away with."

"So he thinks the Burk kid is one of the guys who robbed him?"

"That's what he thinks."

"You send anyone up to investigate?"

"Yeah, Brian and Buck."

"Good choice. Pugh is the best we've got, and Buck can come in handy if things get rough."

"I just got a call from Pugh and they're headed over to the Burks' place to talk to Milo."

"I know Milo. He used to be a pretty decent kid, straight-A all the way through grade school and high school. Then his folks sent him off to college. He flunked out his first semester and has run wild ever since. Never send a kid to college! That's where Milo started drinking and fighting. There's no telling what he and his friends might do. I hope Pugh knows that."

"Yeah, he does. And in case you've forgotten, you went to college."

"Yeah, but I was an art major. And look at me now."

Daisy laughed. "Well, I told Brian to be careful."

Tully snorted. "A lot of good that will do, knowing Pugh like I do. He'll probably try to bring Milo in by himself. Well, it sounds as if you've got everything under control, Daisy. I'll finish business up here and then head in."

He clicked off. Clyde Parker. If anything deserved to be robbed it was Clyde's General Store. It had been robbing the residents of Pine Flats blind for thirty years. If any of them wanted a box of cornflakes, they had to pay Clyde twice the normal price or drive forty miles to the nearest town to buy it. On the other hand, Milo Burk was a tough kid and could be dangerous. He hoped Pugh would pay attention to Daisy's warning. One thing for sure, the robbers were poor. Poor people rob you with a gun, a knife, or a club, and rich people rob you with a pen or a cash register. Tully wasn't sure which kind of robber was the more dangerous.

Chapter 3

The back road to the Fester ranch was rough, icy, and rutted with snow, forcing Tully to put the Explorer into four-wheel-drive. He soon emerged from the rolling hills, and the forest gradually thinned into open ranchlands. A large herd of black-and-white cows grazed near a fence where bales of hay had been broken and dumped out for them. The tracks of the truck that had dumped the bales turned in the field and made their way back to a gate in the fence near the road. Suddenly Tully had a nice flat surface of snow to drive on the rest of his way to the ranch. He finally reached the headquarters, where someone had plowed the entrance-road snow down almost to gravel. The main ranch house was dark and still, so he continued on behind it to a huge bunkhouse, where smoke rose from the chimney and lights glowed in the windows. A dozen or so pickup trucks were parked in an area next to the bunkhouse. He got out and pounded on the door. A bearded young man dressed in jeans and a faded red underwear top opened it. "Yeah?"

"Sir, I'm Blight County Sheriff Bo Tully. I wonder if I might ask you and the other members of your crew some questions."

"What if I say no?"

Tully pulled back his coat front to show his badge. "In that case, son, I knock you on your butt and ask my questions anyway. And I better get some good answers."

The kid stepped back. "Come on in." He shouted over his shoulder. "Jeff, there's a cop here to see you!"

A voice growled from the back of the barracks. "Well, show him in, Wiggens. I'll be right out."

Four other ranch hands sat around a table playing cards. A couple of them nodded at Tully and then went on with their game. Tully glanced into a large room off to his right. A pool table sat in the middle of it and a large flat-screen television loomed at the far end. He guessed bunkhouses had improved quite a bit over the years.

A door opened and a small but sturdy man came out combing back his wet thick black hair, apparently having just gotten out of a shower. *Rather small to be ramrodding a crew of ranch hands,* Tully thought. The man strolled over, his cowboy boots thudding on the board floor, and stuck out his hand. "Sheriff, I'm Jeff Sheridan. I'm in charge of the ranch while the boss is gone."

Tully shook his hand. Sheridan scarcely came up past his shoulder. He was slim and handsome. Even ranch foremen apparently had changed a lot over the years. "Actually, Mr. Sheridan, I'm here to ask you about your boss."

"I'm afraid I can't tell you much. Mr. Fester doesn't, exactly confide in me."

Tully took off his hat and ran his fingers back through his hair. "Maybe I'm the one to tell you something, Mr. Sheridan. Morgan Fester is dead."

The man dealing cards at the table stopped. The foreman sucked in his breath. "Dead! No wonder I haven't heard from him. We thought he'd packed up and gone off to his ranch in Mexico, without bothering to tell us. Not entirely unlike him. One day he was just gone, without saying a word or giving us any orders or anything. He left the same day as Mrs. Sheridan. He'd been talking about leaving for a while but never bothered to discuss his plans with us. We thought probably he had left with the missus. How do you know he's dead?"

"Found his body on a knoll just off South River Road, a little past Trapper Creek."

The men at the table had stopped playing cards and were staring at the two of them.

Tully stared back. "How long did you say he's been gone?"

Sheridan scratched his chin. "Three weeks or so, I'd guess, since the time Mrs. Fester left for Mexico. I might be able to tell you the exact day, if I check his office. It's over in their house."

"I don't think this is an emergency, but I would like to find a phone number for Mrs. Fester. I understand she's spending the winter in Cabo San Lucas. She probably gave her husband a number where she's staying. Think we could take a look?"

"Sure. I'll grab the key." He walked into a side room that looked like a small office of some kind and lifted a key off a bulletin board containing numerous other keys.

They stomped through the snow over toward the ranch house. Tully suddenly stopped and said, "Whoa! That's the largest bird feeder I've ever seen!"

Sheridan smiled. "Mrs. Fester is quite the lover of wildlife. One of our main jobs in winter is to keep that feeder full at all times. You see the path that leads over to that thicket of brush and trees?"

"Yeah, I thought there might be an old outhouse or something in there."

"Nope, a big covey of quail winters in there. Mrs. Fester expects me to keep that path shoveled out so the quail don't have to walk through snow on their way to the feeder."

Tully laughed. "I've heard of bird lovers, but this seems a bit extreme."

"That's nothing. For a while we were feeding half the deer in Blight County over the winter, but finally Mr. Fester put his foot down and said no more of that. I guess he wasn't about to go up against her when it came to birds, though."

They went up on the porch and stomped the snow off their boots. Tully glanced at the parking lot. "Your hands definitely seem to favor pickups. Not a sports car in the lot."

Sheridan laughed. "Sports cars are much too sissy for these guys. All three-quarter-ton four-wheel-drives. Most of them belong to the crew, but several are owned by the ranch."

"Fester drive any of those owned by the ranch?"

"Yeah, any he wanted. I don't think he had a particular favorite."

"Interesting. How about Mrs. Fester?"

Sheridan studied the pickups in the lot. "Well, she favored a big green truck, but I don't see it. I don't know whether she owns it or the ranch does. Same difference, I guess. C'mon in. I'll show you their house."

He turned the key in the lock and opened the door, and they went in. The living room was richly furnished, dominated by a huge flat-screen TV. *Those things are practically ubiquitous,* Tully thought, pleased at having remembered the word. He wished he had said it out loud for Sheridan's benefit. The foreman led Tully down a hallway paneled in dark wood of some kind. "Mr. Fester's office is right here," Sheridan said, taking out a key and unlocking the door. The office was large and had a huge metal desk. A leather couch stretched halfway across one wall. The foreman checked a pad by the phone. Several phone numbers were printed on it, followed by names. "That must be hers," he said, pointing to a number with the name "Hil" after it.

Tully took out his pen and pocket notebook and wrote down the number. "Thanks. I'll get in touch with Mrs. Fester. I'm sure you'll hear from her, but I'll let you know what we turn up. By the way, can you tell me how they got along?"

Sheridan hesitated. "Okay, I guess. He let her do whatever she wanted, and he did what he wanted. He got upset with her from time to time, though, and would give her a pop."

A pop? Tully imagined an orange soda and was horrified at such cruelty.

Sheridan went on. "Yeah, ever so often she would show up with a black eye. Riled the crew no end. They would have lynched Mr. Fester if I let them, and I was tempted sometimes. She's much younger than him, beautiful and very gentle and nice, but she can be feisty, too. She's plenty smart. I think every one of the crew is in love with her. You could find several good suspects for his murder right here on the ranch, Sheriff."

"Sounds like quite the lady."

"Yeah, she is. I never understood why she put up with Mr. Fester. Maybe that's why she spends half the year in Mexico."

"You ever visit the ranch down there?"

"Yeah, I do. Mr. Fester sends me down there several times a year. Ranching isn't what it used to be, Sheriff. You'd expect someone like me to be out breaking broncos and branding steers, but I'll show you where I do most of my work, when I'm not running off rustlers."

He led Tully down the hallway and opened a door. They went in. "This little office is mine, where most of the work gets done." He pointed to a computer on a desk and a swivel chair. "There's the bronco I ride and the herd I drive, Sheriff. Sometimes seems as if I'm in that saddle all day and half the night."

Tully smiled. "And here I've always wanted to be a ranch foreman. You do much with the Mexican ranch?"

"Quite a bit, at least on the computer. That's some spread. Makes this one look like a gopher colony. Mr. Fester's idea was that one day he would have me manage that one, too. He even hired the Spanish teacher at the Blight City High School to teach me the language. So I already know *un poco español*."

"Sounds as if you and I know about the same amount. Maybe we had the same teacher. So what do you think Mrs. Fester will do with the Mexican ranch?"

Sheridan shook his head. "I have no idea. She likes Mexico a lot and unlike me speaks fluent Spanish. I wouldn't be surprised if she sold this one and kept that one."

"One last thing. Do Mr. and Mrs. Fester share a bedroom or do they each have a separate one?"

Sheridan frowned. "Well, they do have separate ones."

"Would it be all right if I took a look in Mrs. Fester's bedroom?" He interpreted the look on Sheridan's face as implying, "This sheriff is one weird dude."

"I guess so," the foreman said. He pushed open another door.

Tully walked in, looking around. The bed was neatly made and the furnishings extremely plush. "Okay if I look in her closet?"

Sheridan shook his head, apparently in disbelief, but then said, "Sure, go ahead." Tully slid back the closet doors and peered down at the shelves beneath the clothing. They contained dozens of pairs of footwear, about every kind imaginable. He had never seen so many shoes except in a shoe store. "Mrs. Fester much of an outdoors person?"

"Oh, yeah, she loves hiking in the woods and mountains, usually going out by herself. Sometimes she camps out alone. Used to drive the boys crazy but didn't seem to bother Mr. Fester much. I don't think there's a single wild plant or bird she doesn't know the scientific name of. She picks a lot of huckleberries and wild mushrooms and sometimes brings us huckleberry pies or big skillets of fried mushrooms. They are scrumptious! I tell you, Sheriff, she is one terrific lady."

Tully held out his hand. "Sounds like it, Mr. Sheridan. Thanks for the information and for showing me around. If I learn anything about Fester's murder, I'll give you a call." Sheridan's grip was stronger than he had expected, for someone who rode a chair and wrangled a computer. "Oh, by the way, Jeff, can you tell me the day Mrs. Fester left for Mexico?"

"Yeah, it was December third."

"Thanks, I appreciate it."

"You got any suspects, Sheriff?"

"Yeah, the whole town of Silver Tip, to start with. Oh, one last thing. I'd expect that Mrs. Fester's being such a lover of nature, she would have at least one pair of hiking boots in her closet. I didn't see any."

Sheridan looked puzzled. "That's odd, Sheriff. I know she has a pair. She wears them half the time.

She loves to explore out in the desert, though, and probably took them to Mexico with her."

"Thanks for all your help, Mr. Sheridan. I'll keep you informed about our investigation and you can pass along to Mrs. Fester anything you think might interest her or might suggest to her something that would help us solve this murder."

"You bet, Sheriff."

Tully started to leave but suddenly stopped and turned around. "Oh, by the way, Mr. Sheridan, does Mrs. Fester have a room where she works on hobbies or anything like that?"

"Why yes, she does, Sheriff. She had it built as an attachment to the back of the house, so it could be furnished with heat, water, and lights from the house. She spends a lot of time working on her hobbies in there. Would you like to see it? I don't think she would mind."

"Yes, I would."

Sheridan led him back through the house to a cozy room obviously added on to the house and with an entrance from the enclosed back porch. Several tables held neat stacks of cloth. A workbench along one side contained a variety of tools that might be used for tasks Tully had not a clue about. One little instrument in particular caught his attention, a vice of some sort, but for what purpose he had no idea. "Well, Mr. Sheridan, it appears that Mrs. Fester is one talented lady. I can't even guess what all these instruments and tools are for."

"Me neither, Sheriff. She has a room just about like this one down at the Mexico ranch. In fact, she seems like a very happy lady, particularly when her husband isn't around. And from what you tell me, I guess he won't be anymore."

Tully nodded. "Yeah, Morg Fester is history. In any case, I will try to get in touch with Mrs. Fester, pass along the bad news, and find out what her plans are for returning to the ranch."

Sheridan walked him out to the Explorer. As Tully started to climb in, he glanced at a barn some distance from the house. He turned to Sheridan. "What's that big green round thing hanging on the side of the barn?"

Sheridan turned and frowned. "Oh that." He laughed and shook his head. "That's some of Mrs. Fester's doing. She thinks cows should have a Christmas too. The green thing is a big wreath. She decorates that whole barn with lights and trimmings for Christmas. Last year she had a truckload of apples hauled in and dumped in a pasture for the cows, a Christmas present for them! I expect she has something like that on order for their Christmas this year, too, but I haven't heard anything."

"Cows eat apples?"

"They loved these. You ever see a cow smile, Sheriff?"

"No, and I don't want to. Well, thanks for your help, Mr. Sheridan. I'll let you know if I turn up any evidence related to the murder."

"I'd appreciate that."

After leaving Sheridan, Tully drove up the road for a dozen miles, looking the ranch over. The place was gigantic. One feedlot contained what must have been a couple hundred cows, Tully estimated, with two hands rolling bales of hay off a flatbed truck to feed them. After turning around, he headed back to the knoll. So far there seemed to be no shortage of suspects in the murder of Morg Fester. Tully doubted any of his cowhands had undertaken the task. They didn't seem that energetic or ambitious. There simply wasn't that much of an upside for one of them to kill the boss, as far as he could tell.

Chapter 4

When Tully came to the knoll, his CSI unit was already out processing the site. The Explorer slid to a stop and he radioed the office. Florence answered.

"Hi, Flo. Get me Daisy, please."

"She's right here, Boss."

Daisy came on. "Yeah, Bo?"

"Daisy, any word about what's happening with the robbery in Pine Flats?"

"Nothing yet."

Tully thought for a moment. "I have to check with Lurch to see what he's come up with on Fester's murder, and then I'll head up to Pine Flats first thing tomorrow. So I probably won't come into the office today. I'm a little worried about that Burk kid. He's been pretty wild ever since he flunked out of college. No crimes that I know of, but he makes a good suspect in some of the weird stuff that's been going on up around Pine

Flats. If you talk to Pugh and Toole, tell them to stay on their toes. That robbery could turn into a nasty business."

"Gotcha, Boss."

Tully hung up, got out, and looked around the crime scene. The Unit was standing over next to the woods. "You and Pap find anything, Lurch?" he yelled.

"Some stuff, Boss!" He plodded over to Tully. "Pap is pretty amazing when it comes to tracking. But I don't know if what we found means anything." He too displayed no clue he had ever worn snowshoes. "The body was lying on a foot of snow that had frozen and crusted over sometime after Fester was killed. The crusted snow left a pretty good imprint of the body. The snow falling when Fester was killed amounted to about eight inches, about six inches of it on the victim. That was the second snow of the year and should give us a good estimate of the time Fester was killed. I'll check the weather reports at the TV station when I get back to see what I can come up with for time of the first snow in this area. I doubt the ME can do any better than that for time of death."

"Very good, Lurch. Anything else?"

"Now we get into extreme guessing, Boss. I checked the body at the ME's and calculated that to shoot our man in the back, the killer had to shoot from the edge of the woods directly behind him. Dimples in the latest snow indicate it filled in tracks coming out of the woods and going back in. Pap pointed that out. The distance from the tracks to the body was almost exactly twenty yards. If the shooter had driven up in a vehicle on the road, the victim probably would have turned around and been looking at him. If it seemed to him the guy was going to shoot him, he would have been ducking and dodging and running for cover, in which case he wasn't likely to be shot right in the middle of the back."

Tully nodded. He would have smiled but hated giving Lurch too much encouragement. "So you figure the shooter had been hiding in the woods, stepped out after Fester walked by, and shot him. Anything else?"

"Well, the shooter must have known the vic came by here at a regular time and been waiting for him, meaning he knew Fester pretty well. So Pap and I followed the dimples in the new snow to see where they led. The woods are very thick back in there and there's virtually no wind to move the snow around. We tracked the dimples and found a bump in the snow, dug it out and found several pieces of chopped-up wood, some of it blackened from being burned. I took a piece that wasn't completely burnt, to see if I can get some prints off it, although not likely, given the snow and everything. It kind of indicates the shooter had to wait quite a while for the vic to show up, so he built a fire to keep warm, far enough back in the woods so it and the smoke couldn't be seen from the knoll but close enough he could hear the sound of any vehicle pulling up and stopping. Pap and I suspect the shooter slipped into the other side of the woods about five o'clock or earlier, while it was still dark."

Tully shook his head. "Lurch, you and Pap are absolutely amazing!"

"Thanks, Boss."

"Anyway, I leave it to you to match up the time of the killing with the first snowfall. I'm headed in. Where's Pap, by the way?"

"He headed home. I'd love to track with him again. He didn't seem to mind teaching me some of the stuff he knows."

"I'll see what I can do, Lurch. Pap is kind of an ornery cuss and pretty much does whatever he wants when he wants. Sounds as if he might have liked you. That would make one."

Tully changed his mind about going home and got to the office late in the afternoon. Florence, the radio operator, apparently having heard the *klocking* of his boots approaching, stuck her head out from behind the partition that separated the radio room from the briefing room. "I just put fresh coffee in your thermos, Boss. Should be nice and hot."

Tully took his Picasso thermos off the shelf and filled a cup.

"Thanks, Flo! You got anything to eat back there?"

"Half a combo of Italian pizza. Lots of black olives on top and it's delicious."

"Sounds perfect! You done with it?"

"Yep. I'll hand you the box."

"Wonderful, Flo! Once again you've saved my life. I may give you a raise."

"Any time soon?"

"Probably not while you're young enough to appreciate it."

Florence handed him a large flat box still warm to the touch. After thanking her profusely, he carried the box into his office, opened it on his desk, and sank into his leather-padded office chair with a long sigh. When he had finished the pizza and the last few crumbs in the box, he opened his pocket notebook and dialed the number inside.

A man answered in Spanish.

Tully asked, "*Usted habla inglés?*"

"Si," the man replied. "What can I do for you, Señor?"

"Do you have a lady registered there by the name of Mrs. Morgan Fester?"

"We do not give out the names of our guests over the telephone, Señor. If you give me your name and number, I will give her your message and maybe she will call you back."

"If you can do that as quickly as possible, sir, I will greatly appreciate it. This is Sheriff Bo Tully in Blight City, Idaho. I have some bad news for her. Ask her to please call me at her earliest convenience." He gave the man his office phone number.

Daisy buzzed him a few minutes later. "Hillory Fester on line two, Boss."

He picked up. "Mrs. Fester?"

"Yes, Sheriff."

"Mrs. Fester, I'm afraid I have some bad news for you regarding your husband."

"Oh, I already know. It was quite a shock. Jeff Sheridan called and told me about your visit. I asked myself who on earth would want to kill Morgan. But then so many people came to mind, I was a bit overwhelmed."

"I would certainly like to see a list of those people, Mrs. Fester. Please write down the names and the reason each might want to kill him, if you happen to know. I realize that's a lot to ask, right after you've heard such terrible news."

She burst out in a bitter laugh. "Sheriff, I'm afraid my own name would top the list. Maybe the reason I've never killed him, he gave me all the money I wanted and let me do whatever I could think of. He, of course, did whatever he wanted. I don't know how many girl-friends he had, but I know some of their names. I'll write them down for you. Their boyfriends and hus-bands might be good suspects. While you're waiting for my list, you might start with that brothel in Silver Tip. It was his favorite hangout."

"Silver Tip? Yes, I'll check it out. Anyway, Mrs. Fester, I'm sorry to be a bearer of bad tidings."

"*Hillory*, please, Sheriff. And let's just refer to the tiding as tidings. I'll be back in a few days to check on the ranch and the boys and make funeral arrange-ments. Jeff Sheridan is perfectly capable of running the ranch on his own, but he may need my support."

"I think he has everything under control, Ma'am. As you know, I stopped by and talked to him earlier today."

"Yes, I know. The whole crew is a fine lot, and Jeff in particular. He's very intelligent, Sheriff. And thought-ful, too."

"I'm sure he is. In any case, I'll look forward to meet-ing you when you get back. And don't forget that list."

She gave another little laugh. "I'm writing it in my head as we speak."

Tully said good-bye and hung up.

His secretary walked over from her desk and stood in the doorway. "Hillory didn't seem too broken up to hear somebody killed her husband."

Tully nodded. "Actually, I think it made her day. It's as if a whole new world of opportunity has suddenly opened up for her, without the irritation of an ornery husband second-guessing her. I'd better check out the one lead she gave me."

"Oh, by all means," Daisy said. "You'll definitely want to check out Silver Tip."

"Yes, indeed. And since you listen to all my phone calls, Daisy, maybe you could just answer them and save me the trouble."

"Funny, I've been thinking the same thing."

"Any word from Buck or Brian?"

"Yeah, they've got several leads and one good one. Brian said they're going to spend the night at the Pine Flats Motel."

"Okay. Get in touch with them and tell them I'll be up tomorrow and will meet them at the café for lunch."

Chapter 5

It was already dark as Tully drove into the parking lot of the Silver Tip Hotel, a well-aged, four-story brick structure on the edge of town. A thick new-growth forest of fir trees descended the mountain directly behind the hotel and embraced it and its parking lot on three sides. For a moment Tully thought he might sink to the ground from exhaustion, but he managed to walk over to the main entrance of the hotel and ring the doorbell. A burly bald man raised some slats in a venetian blind over the door and peered out. Then he unlocked the door and pushed it open. "My goodness, Bo, what brings you out our way?"

"Just looking for some information, Ed, and this is usually a good place to find some."

"You try the library?"

"Doesn't have the kind of information I'm looking for. Maggie available?"

"You know she's always available to you, Bo. Have a seat and I'll give her a call."

Tully plopped into one of the red plush chairs that lined one side of the entranceway. Ed picked up a phone, dialed a number, and said, "Bo Tully to see you, Maggie." He listened, then hung up and turned to Tully. "She'll be right down, Bo. Like a drink while you're waiting?"

"Yeah, I would. Unfortunately, I can't, since I'm here strictly on business."

"Sounds serious."

"Afraid it is. Murder."

Ed shook his head. "That *is* serious. Anyone we know?"

"That's what I'm here to find out."

Maggie came strutting across the hardwood floor leading to the entrance area, her high heels clicking smartly on the polished wood, her auburn hair perfectly done, the tight-fitting red dress fairly shouting "high-end boutique." Her green eyes sparkled with amusement behind rimless glasses. "Sheriff Tully! Nice to see you up our way, Bo. Ed, get the sheriff something to drink." She held out her hand. Tully stood up and gave it a squeeze.

"Already offered, Maggie, but Bo says he's here on duty. He's investigating a crime."

"Oh, that's a shame. What can I do for you, Bo?"

"We've had a rather nasty murder, Maggie, and I'm told by the wife of the victim that he liked to hang out here quite a lot."

Maggie frowned. "Well, as you know, Bo, this is a hotel catering to respectable and well-educated professional ladies who rent our rooms. I don't inquire about any private transactions they may undertake. Gentlemen from all over the country come here in search of intelligent conversation. In fact, they make a point of traveling out of their way, just to stop by Silver Tip."

Tully smiled. "I think some of them might even be federal lawmen looking for bad guys. I suppose they don't bother to ask about your ladies' private transactions."

"No, they don't. But for your information, Sheriff, the main thing our ladies sell is attention. Men come here just because the ladies listen to their stories and jokes and lies so attentively."

"I thought that must be the case. So what can you tell me about Morgan Fester?" He settled back in his chair.

"Somebody killed Morg?"

"Afraid so. I thought maybe some idiot might have stopped by here and bragged about the killing. Been known to happen."

Maggie slid into the chair next to Tully and lit a cigarette, tucking her silver lighter away in a pocket of her dress. "Yes, it has. This is the first I've heard about Morg, though. There are folks around here who would view his killing as a service to the community." She inhaled deeply and blew out a stream of smoke. "I haven't heard anything, Bo, but I'll ask the ladies. I know Morg favored Sasha in particular. She's very attentive, and I'm sure Morg told her all sorts of stuff, maybe some of it even true. That happens sometimes." She turned to her doorman. "Ed, call Sasha and tell her a gentleman in the lobby would like to speak to her."

"You referring to Bo?"

"Yes, I am! Now shut up and call Sasha." She turned back to Tully. "For heaven's sake, Bo, don't ask her about birds."

"I wasn't intending to. Why?"

"She'll talk your arm off about birds. Oh, she is a nut when it comes to our fine feathered friends. Travels all over the world, spotting and photographing rare species."

"All over the world? She must be independently wealthy."

"Could be. She gets paid extremely well here, let me tell you, and she also gets free room and board and some help with the expense of her travels. She's worth every penny I spend on her, though. You know Augie Finn, I'm sure."

Tully grimaced. "Yeah, I know Augie well. He and his newspaper have been thorns in my side for years. How do you know him?"

"Oh, he stops by every couple of weeks to check on us. He's even done several features on some of the ladies who live here."

"Yes, I read his stories about the ladies and enjoyed them. I must admit he's a major pain in my life, but I do like his writing."

"Several of our ladies do some very nice crafts, like knitting and patchwork quilts, and one even does oil paintings. Augie has written stories on nearly all of them, even mentioning their place of residence. He says some of his readers are surprised the ladies seem so normal and interesting. A month or so ago he did a feature on Sasha and her interest in birds. It was a fantastic story and very funny."

Tully nodded. "I read it. I guess I didn't make the connection with this Silver Tip at the time. I hate to admit it, but I read everything Augie writes. I'm not fond of his stories about me and my investigations, though. He's a funny guy and never lets a mere fact stand in the way of a good piece. His writing reminds me of Mark Twain. Most of the time, though, he's a pain in my backside. The reporters in my own town, at the *Blight City Daily News,* are so ignorant and lazy I never have to worry about them. They'll print any tidbit I give them. But Augie and that miserable little *Silver Tip Miner* drive me nuts. I think everybody in Blight County who knows how to read never misses an edition. What was the bird lady's name again?"

"Sasha. I never give out last names of the ladies. You'll have to get that from her, if she wants to give it. Morg was particularly fond of Sasha. As you probably know, he owns—or owned—two huge ranches."

"Yeah," Tully said. "I've known Morg a long time. I guess I'm one of the few people in the county who actually liked the guy. He reminded me of my grandfather."

"Really? I'm sorry."

"Yeah, old Gramps was as nasty a piece of work as ever set foot in Blight County. Morgan Fester didn't fall much short of his record, though."

"Oh, dear! Well, here comes Sasha. I'd better scoot and leave you two alone to talk. By the way, Bo, have you eaten supper yet? You look famished."

"Now that you mention it, I could use a bite."

A sturdy but pretty blond woman walked up. Maggie introduced her to Tully. He noticed she had a very firm grip when she shook his hand.

Maggie said, "Sasha, do you know if we have any of that roast beef left from supper? The sheriff is starving to death right here in front of us."

Sasha smiled. "He's in luck. I'll bring him back a platter." She left and disappeared into a side room.

"You'll like Sasha," Maggie said. "She's your kind of people."

"My kind?" Tully said.

"Yeah, she likes to fish and hunt. She keeps us well supplied with wild fish and game."

"I suppose you know that using venison commercially is illegal, not that there's anything wrong with that, Maggie."

She laughed. "Of course I do, Sheriff. But we only serve it free to our guests. There's nothing wrong with serving venison free to guests, is there?"

"I suppose not."

Maggie said, "Come with me, Bo. You'll like eating in our dining room better than out here." She led him into a spacious room filled with white-linen-covered tables, crystal chandeliers, large mirrors on the walls, and other elegant features a first-time visitor wouldn't expect to find in a grimy little mining town like Silver Tip. Presently, Sasha came in carrying a tray. It held a platter heaped with slabs of dark meat and a small mountain of mashed potatoes, all of it covered with dark brown gravy, next to a side of grilled vegetables, another side of thick toasted bread slices, and a salad. She pulled up a small table with her foot and set the platter down in front of Tully. The aroma almost brought tears to his eyes. Sasha said, "I had to warm the roast and potatoes in the microwave. Sorry about that. Hope it's all right, Sheriff."

Tully nodded and dug in. When he had finished devouring every last morsel, he ran a finger across the empty plate and licked it off, the only bit of gravy he had missed. Maggie and Sasha were smiling at him. He felt embarrassed. "I hope you didn't get splattered," he said, "but that's the best meal I've eaten in my entire life!"

Maggie grinned. "I'm so glad we could be of service."

Tully smiled at her. "Thanks for being so attentive to my eating, Maggie."

"You're welcome, Bo, even if you are a smart aleck."

Tully stood up and pulled over the nearest chair for Sasha. She sat, smoothing her stained white slacks as she did so. "Sorry for the way I look, Sheriff. I was about to take a shower but didn't think you'd want to wait until I got spiffed up."

"You look great to me," he said, sitting back down. "And call me Bo. Everybody around here does."

Maggie said, "I'll leave you two to your discussion. I've got some work I'd better take care of."

Tully thanked her and she walked back toward her office.

Sasha said, "Well, Sheriff, what can I do for you?"

He cleared his throat. "First I want to mention how impressed I was that your cook was able to imitate the taste of venison so perfectly with those slices of roast beef you served me."

She smiled. "I guess maybe it's all part of the art of cooking. Actually, Sheriff, it was the final bit of the very last deer I will ever shoot in my life. And I shot it early in the season, in case you're wondering."

"Your last deer. Why is that?"

"Because I've given up killing things. Something happened a while back that made it occur to me that all life wants to live. It doesn't make any difference what form the life takes, something the size of an elephant or of a tiny red spider or a person, it all wants to live."

"A tiny red spider?"

Sasha laughed. "Yeah, a tiny red spider. I was sitting at my desk one day and happened to glance down and there was this group of tiny red spiders watching me. I could see their eyes! And I hate spiders. When they saw I was watching them, they all rushed under a sheet of paper next to my computer. Then they gathered in a little red line and stood there staring out at me from under the sheet of paper, apparently thinking they were hidden. I was about to thump my thumb up and down on top of the paper and squish them when it occurred to me that even life in the form and size of a tiny spider wants to live. So right then and there I made up my mind never to kill anything again."

Tully smiled. "But Maggie told me you love to fish."

"I did, Sheriff, but I don't anymore. You know why a fish fights so hard when it's hooked?"

"Hmm. Actually, Sasha, I haven't thought that much about it."

"It's because the fish feels helpless and is terrified by the unknown force pulling against it. The fish doesn't want to die."

Tully sighed. "Well, there you go, Sasha. You just ruined fishing for me. Fortunately, fly fishing is finished around here until spring, and I should be over this conversation by then."

She laughed. "I didn't mean to ruin fishing for you, Sheriff. It's just a silly idea of mine. I go through periods of being weird, but I usually get over it."

Tully stood up to go. "Well, I've enjoyed our conversation, but I had better head back to the station. Or better yet, home."

"Come again soon, Sheriff. It was fun talking to you."

"You, too. By the way, Maggie tells me Morgan Fester enjoyed talking to you, and I happen to know men often blab stuff to attentive ladies they wouldn't want anybody else to know."

"Well, I'll tell you this," Sasha said. "Morg Fester is a nasty piece of work."

"Morg is past tense, Sasha. He *was* a nasty piece of work. Now he is a dead piece of work. Somebody murdered him."

"No!"

"Yes. I was hoping you might be able to tell me if Fester ever mentioned anything to you about somebody wanting to kill him."

Sasha thought for a moment. "No, and I would remember something like that. I suspect any number of people would be pleased to see him dead but wouldn't want to do the deed themselves. His wife might be high up on that list, but I understand she's quite a nice person, goes off and does her own thing and never speaks ill of Morg. They're rich and she can do just about anything she wants. Morg told me she spends the winter in Cabo San Lucas. I guess they have another big ranch in Mexico. Did you know Morg was fluent in Spanish?"

"I didn't know about the Spanish. I knew he was smart."

Sasha smiled. "I don't know many smart people, except maybe those government agents who stop by every few months tracking some gangster. And now you, of course."

"Yeah, I stop by occasionally myself. Get some of my best leads here. Well, I'm sorry to keep you from your shower, Sasha. Actually, I'm not. It's a pleasure meeting you. By the way, you seem quite different from the other ladies."

Sasha laughed. "I don't know if that's a compliment, Sheriff. The ladies are all pretty nice."

"I know they are. Take care, Sasha."

He got up and headed for the door. Ed was there and unlocked it for him. "That Sasha's something, ain't she, Bo?"

"She is that, Ed. My head is still spinning."

"I hope you didn't get her talking on birds."

"No, Maggie had warned me about birds. I have to say, though, there's something about Sasha that's different from the other ladies."

"Oh, that's because she ain't one of the ladies, Bo. She spends most of her time in the kitchen. Sasha's the chef. Almost never comes out front but occasionally does chat with some of the guests."

"You mean she cooked that wonderful meal I just ate?"

"Yep. She keeps us all pretty well fed, even Morgan Fester from time to time. Her and Fester used to get into terrible rows."

"Fester? About what?"

"Oh, mostly eagles. I guess eagles killed a calf of his once and ate it. Probably had a hundred wolf tracks around the kill, but he blamed the eagles. Morg hates eagles. He's got a thousand head of cattle but apparently prized that one calf over all the rest. Well, as you probably know by now, Sasha's got a thing about birds, eagles topping the list."

"That's what I understand."

"Yeah, she loves birds. Kind of fanatical about them, if you ask me. When she's got enough money saved up, she plans on going back to college to get a degree in birds. She's already got a master's degree in biology, but I guess there aren't a lot of jobs out there for women with a master's degree in biology."

"So she wants to be an ornithologist?"

"Good heavens, no! She ain't into any of that weird stuff. She just wants to study birds. I'm pretty sure Maggie plans to pay for her college. Bo, we do get a passel of weird women here."

"Sounds like it. Well, thanks for the info." He started to walk out but then noticed something hanging out of one of the man's rear pockets. "Say, Ed, that isn't a blackjack, is it?"

Ed looked surprised. "What? A blackjack? Oh, good heavens, no, Bo. Ha! I think that would be illegal." He pulled the leather object out of his hip pocket. "Well, what this is, I just recently got into loading my own shotgun shells. And I carry the lead shot in this little leather bag. Oh, sure, once in a while a couple customers will get involved in a bit of a brawl, and I give one or both of them a tap with my little leather shot bag. It has a wonderful soothing effect. Calms them right down."

"I bet it does. It seems like something I could use from time to time."

Ed tossed the little leather bag back and forth in his hands. "Tell you what, Bo. I have another one at home just like it. You can have this one if you like." He held it out.

Tully took the little bag with one hand and slapped it a couple of times into the palm of his other hand. It was surprisingly heavy for its size. "Why, thank you, Ed, I appreciate it."

"No problem, Bo. You thinking of loading your own shotgun shells?"

"Something like that."

Chapter 6

After pulling out of the brothel's parking lot, Tully turned toward the business section of Silver Tip. He cruised slowly down Main Street, checking out the storefronts on each side. Then he saw it, a rather dilapidated frame building but with a neatly painted sign on a small front window that said THE SILVER TIP MINER. He made a U-turn at the next intersection, drove back, and parked next to the newspaper office. A light glowed dimly in the back, indicating perhaps someone might still be at work there, maybe Augie himself. He got out and rapped on the window with one knuckle. A man in a white beard and mustache and wearing a full-length leather apron put a hand to his eyes, apparently to see if he recognized the person disturbing him. Then he walked to the front of the shop and opened the door.

"My goodness, Sheriff Tully! What brings you prowling around this hour of the night?"

"Sorry to disturb you, sir, but I'm looking for your editor and reporter, the famous August Finn."

The man frowned. "I hope you ain't intending to arrest August over something he wrote about you, Sheriff."

Tully laughed. "Sir, I would be absolutely delighted to arrest August for something, but I'll be darned if I can come up with any law he's broken."

The old man held out his hand. "Vernon Scott's the name, Sheriff. I've read a lot about you in my own *Silver Tip Miner*. But as long as you're not here to arrest my reporter, I'll show you around my newspaper, if you're interested."

"I'd be very interested, Vernon. Can't say I've ever seen any paper quite like the *Silver Tip Miner*."

The editor frowned. "That's because there ain't none like it anywhere in the world. Every other paper I know has gone sissy. We, on the other hand, print everything that's fit to print and quite a bit that ain't. August handles most of the reporting and I run the shop. If you'd like, Sheriff, I'll show you around. I'm kind of proud of our operation, one of the last of its kind in the world."

Tully followed the old printer into his back room. Huge pieces of equipment filled the place.

"My goodness!" Tully said. "Don't tell me I'm looking at a flatbed press!"

"Yes, sir, you are. This here is a flatbed cylinder press, the last of its kind in use, far as I know. Years ago, when all the other weekly newspapers started switching to those sissy offset presses, I went around the country picking up letterpress equipment wherever I could find it. Got most of it for just hauling it away. Of course, they're not making any more of it nowadays, so I figured if some of my machinery broke down I'd want some way to repair or replace it. Now I've got a barn out back of my house crammed full of old letterpress equipment."

Tully shook his head in amazement. "Vernon, I'm surprised you can find any paper around to fit your press."

"Oh, you'd be surprised, Sheriff. There's quite a few folks around who run letterpress as a hobby, print books and stuff like that. We're one of a few, maybe the only one, that prints a regular newspaper. Folks all over miss their letterpress newspapers. I tell you, our readers are absolutely crazy about Augie's writing, think he's Mark Twain come again. You'd be surprised the number of subscribers we have scattered all over the country who get their subscriptions by mail and even some outside the country who get their subscriptions that way, but it doesn't make any difference to them because what they're after is August's writing. You probably noticed we even get some national advertising."

"I have noticed that, Vernon, and wondered about it. Anyway, the reason I stopped by is, I'm looking for August. Can you tell me where I might find him?"

The newspaperman scratched his stubbly chin. "You sure you ain't intending to arrest him?"

"No, much as I would like to, I'm not going to arrest him."

"In that case, he's up at Pine Flats."

"No! Not Pine Flats!"

"Yup, he heard there was a robbery up there and went up to cover it. That's what a real newspaper reporter does."

Tully sighed. "I suppose you're right, Vernon. I'm headed up that way tomorrow and maybe I can catch up with him. Thanks for showing me around the *Silver Tip Miner*."

He walked out to his car and started the long drive home.

Chapter 7

Tully's Explorer bumped down the snowy ruts of the road across the wind-burnished snow of his hayfield, the dark shape of his two-story log house slowly appearing in the glow of his headlights. In the bottomland off to his left wound Grouse Creek, filled with trout in the spring and summer, spawning kokanee salmon in the fall and winter. On the hillside off to his right, a thick woods rose up tall and dark, a half-mile square of mature cedar, pine, larch, tamarack, birch, alder, and an excess of cottonwood. The forest gave him a strange sense of comfort, even though he did practically nothing with it, except for an occasional stroll among the trees.

He and his wife, Ginger, had built the house themselves with logs they had harvested from the forest. They excavated a gigantic hole with hand shovels, poured a concrete floor, and then built stone-and-concrete walls for the basement and foundation, all of it backed with layers of black plastic sheeting to prevent the intrusion of water. To build the log walls, they created an elaborate hoisting system consisting of a tall pole rising straight up from the center of the basement, with a leveraged pole on top rigged with tackle extending out over the construction site. This rather perilous contraption allowed just the two of them to hoist and set log after log in place. After three years of work, the house was completed. And then Ginger died. He felt extremely guilty about her death, thinking maybe it was all the hard work that had killed her, but her doctor said no, it was a congenital weakness in her heart, something she had either been unaware of or had simply chosen to ignore.

Tully never recovered from her death. His loneliness afterward eventually led to the short but passionate affair with Daisy. He had sworn to himself that he would never again allow himself to fall in love. It was simply too painful, and that very likely was what had led Daisy to give up on the affair.

As he bumped down the driveway closer to the house, he hoped maybe one of the lights would be on, because that would mean Daisy had come out for the evening. No such luck. He shut off the car, waded over to the planked front porch, stomped the snow off his boots, and went inside. The living room was dark and gloomy and cold. After turning on the lights, he opened the door of his wood-burning heater, shoveled out the cold burnt remains of the last evening's fire into a bucket, and then thrust in a wadded-up newspaper, two handfuls of shavings, half a dozen sticks of cedar kindling, and three large pieces of split birch. He touched it all off with his lighter. The birch would burn for the rest of the night, and he would at least be able to get up to a warm house. He went to the bedroom, took off his clothes, and, shivering, put on a sweat suit and climbed into bed. Most nights after work he strolled around his studio checking out the paintings he had in various stages of completion. The studio occupied the entire second story. Someday soon, he hoped, he would somehow become a full-time painter. Tonight, however, he simply climbed into bed. The icy coldness of the sheets shot through his sweat suit as if driven by electricity. *Oh, what the hell*, he thought, and went to sleep.

Chapter 8

The next morning, sitting alone sipping coffee and eating a piece of dry burnt toast, he thought his life had better take a change for the better soon. At forty-eight, he was getting too old to keep fighting criminals day after day. There had been a time when he took a certain satisfaction from throwing bad guys in jail and even sending a few of them off to prison. But anymore he felt mostly sorry for the poor stupid wretches, a bad frame of mind for a sheriff. If he had learned anything over the years, it was that you can't be stupid. The world gobbles up stupid people like so many potato chips. Stupid people usually are poor. It comes with the territory. He shoved a bowl of cold cereal to the other side of the table, got up, and drove to town, stopping at McDonald's for his standard breakfast of Egg McMuffin and coffee. Then he headed for the office, to see if there was any word from Brian or Buck on the Pine Flats situation.

Apparently having heard the *klocking* of his cowboy boots on the marble-chip concrete floor of the courthouse hallway, Daisy looked up from her intense conversation with a pudgy little fellow seated in a chair next to her. The man had curly black hair and rimless glasses and was scribbling furiously on a yellow notepad on his knee. He was the editor and only reporter of the *Silver Tip Miner*.

"Augie!" Tully growled. "What are you doing here?"

"Just my routine job of collecting news for my paper. Anything you would like to add, Sheriff, or must I go with the tidbits I've received from my other sources?"

"Are you by any chance at this very minute sitting next to one of your blabbermouth sources?"

"What! Daisy? By no means, Bo. Daisy wouldn't give me the time of day, would you, Daisy?"

"Certainly not!" Daisy said, shaking her head.

"Yeah, right," Tully growled. "Well, come on in, Augie, and I'll give you the lowdown."

Finn winked at Daisy, got up, and followed Tully into his office, closing the door behind them. He pulled up a chair to Tully's desk, sat down, cleared a little space on the desk, and placed his yellow pad on it. "Not often I get a murder to write about, Bo. Mostly it's babies that just got born and grandmothers visiting from out of town."

Tully almost smiled. He couldn't help but like the guy. He was one of the funniest people Tully knew. He was also a towering intellect, at least compared with

most of the residents of Blight County. Tully sometimes wondered why the little man wasn't reporting
for *The Washington Post* or *The New York Times*. He was
perfectly capable of doing so. Instead he had settled
into the little town of Silver Tip, Idaho, and become
not only its leading intellect but also its most prominent citizen, and a first-rate journalist to boot. The
latter included a constant probing of law enforcement
for any signs of corruption or incompetence. So far,
he had found none. As Tully had once told him, it was
too bad he hadn't been around when Pap Tully was
sheriff. He would have thought he was in heaven. And
Pap probably would have been in prison!

Tully leaned back in his swivel chair, folded his
hands on his belly, and said, "Well, Augie, did your
source in the other room fill you in on all the details
of our recent crime?"

"What source is that, Bo? You mean Daisy? Why,
she never gives me the tiniest tidbit about what goes
on here."

"Yeah, right. So what do you want to know about
our murder?"

Tully filled him in on all the details, the few he knew.
The editor thanked him and got up to go.

"By the way, Augie, how did your pictures turn out?"

"Great, as always. I'm running three in next week's
paper. I can give you a set of all the prints, if you want
them."

"I would love a set of prints. You never know
whether there might be something in one of them that
solves our murder. Oh, by the way, Augie, did you talk

to Brian and Buck when you were up in Pine Flats investigating the robbery?"

"As a matter of fact, I did. We had coffee together at the café. The suspects in the crime had fled the scene, but I did get a lead on where they might be hiding out."

"And where is that?"

"Sorry, Bo, I can't reveal facts in my story until they are published. But I did speak to an eyewitness of the so-called crime."

Daisy stuck her head in the door. "Oh, Bo, you just missed an important phone call."

He stared at her. "I can't even imagine a phone call important enough I would want to get it."

"Well, you'll want to get this one. It was from your agent in Spokane. She was all excited."

Tully leaped up from his chair. "Jean Runyan called?"

"Yes!"

"And she was excited?"

"Yes!"

"I've never known Jean to get excited about any-thing but money. Maybe I should call her back."

Daisy shook her head in exasperation. "If you don't do it this minute and tell me what she wanted, I will have to kill you!"

Augie said, "I'd better leave and let you make your phone call, Bo. You can check with me later about the eyewitness up at Pine Flats. I don't think anybody else knows about her. Oh, and I'll also want to know the details about this phone call from your agent."

He got up and left.

Tully sat back down and dialed Jean Runyan's gallery number in Spokane.

One of the clerks answered. "Runyan's."

"Alice, this is Bo Tully, returning Jean's call."

"Oh, Bo! Hold on a sec and I'll get her for you. This is so exciting you won't believe it!"

"Try me, Alice."

"Jean would kill me if I told you. Hold on, here she comes."

The agent picked up. "Bo, you're not going to believe this."

"If you don't tell me quick, I'll come up there and . . ."

"No need to get violent, Sweetie. The news is that an art buyer from a gallery in Seattle came by and bought that big watercolor of yours, the one of the Blight River with the fall cottonwoods in the background."

"Wonderful! A Seattle gallery. That's practically the big time."

"Yes! And he paid twelve thousand dollars for it! And you laughed when I said I was holding out for ten."

"Wow! Now I have to sit down!"

"I told him I couldn't let it go for ten and he offered twelve. I took that. And he wants more paintings from you!"

"Let me call you back, Jean, after my heart starts beating again." He hung up, leaned back in his swivel chair, and put his boots up on his desk.

Daisy jerked opened his door. "Bo, that's so wonderful! Twelve thousand dollars! Now you can become a full-time painter!"

He tugged on the droopy corner of his mustache. "Not quite yet. I still have a murder to solve. If you're done listening to my phone conversations, hunt down the Spokane phone book and check the Spokane Yellow Pages for any archery stores. I know we don't have any in Blight County. Bows and arrows are a bit too prissy for folks around here."

"You got it, Boss."

Tully walked over to his CSI unit. It was typing madly away on a computer. "Lurch, you and Pap come up with anything more on the person who shot the arrow into our vic?"

The Unit stopped typing and looked up. "Yeah, I did, Boss. If the boot tracks in the woods belong to the shooter, and Pap was pretty sure they do, they had to be made at almost the same time Fester was shot. That's what the snow indicates, anyway. The shooter was a small guy no more than five-eight or so."

"How do you figure that?"

"That's what Pap figured. The tracks were made by a small boot, a size eight at most or even smaller. That would indicate a pretty small man, don't you think?"

"Or maybe an average-size woman," Tully said. He thought about the hiking boots he had expected to see in Hillory Fester's closet but hadn't. He stood up and looked out the window at Lake Blight. It had frozen over and was now covered with several inches of snow. Perfect for ice fishing. Just his luck to be stuck with the stupid murder of someone most sensible people hated anyway. "Yeah, Lurch, it definitely seems as if we're not looking for a giant of any kind in the way of a killer, particularly an intellectual one. How did you find his tracks, anyway?"

"Pap scraped away the top layer of snow and dipped out the prints in the crust of the first snow with a plastic spoon. He showed me how to do it. He's pretty fantastic when it comes to tracking."

Tully shook his head and smiled. The old man hadn't lost his touch. "You find anything that might tie the shooter to the tracks?"

Lurch leaned back in his swivel chair and sighed. "Only that the person who made the tracks in the woods and the vic were at the scene at the same time, right after that first snowfall, in fact right at the start of it."

Tully frowned. "Let's see now, Lurch. Pap's and your theory is that the shooter somehow knew Fester would be showing up on a particular morning at a particular time, apparently to shoot at eagles across the river. From what I've learned about Fester, it's quite likely he was the nut killing eagles. Maybe he bragged about it to someone and that person either became the shooter or told the shooter when Fester would show up. The shooter got to the woods early. While he waited for Fester, he built a fire back in there where it couldn't be seen and was using it to keep warm." He turned from the window and looked back at the Unit. "That the way you see it?"

Lurch nodded. "Yeah. Pap, too. That's what we think the evidence indicates."

"So why didn't the shooter just step out of the woods and drill Fester in the back of the head with a rifle? If he thought a rifle would make too much sound, there's not a house within two miles of the clearing. Hunting season was over, but it's not unusual to hear shots in the woods after the season closes, usually some poacher working late on his winter's venison."

Lurch nodded. "Yeah, I thought about that, too. You want to know how the shooter got to the woods, Boss?"

"Yes, you got any idea?"

"I do. He drove into a little skid trail on the far side of the woods, then hiked into where he built the fire and waited for Fester. That first snow was fresh at the time, still falling, but I was able to get a cast of the tire print and of the boot print leaving it. It's a pretty good cast, good enough for us to find a match. I also got some good photos of the tire's imprint in the ice. There's a place where the tread was nicked pretty hard by something sharp. If we find the tire and match the nick to the imprint of the tread, we can place the owner or at least the driver at the scene and time of the murder. Then I think we've got our killer. Pap figures a four-wheel-drive pickup and, given the tire size, a three-quarter-ton."

Tully shook his head in amazement. "Excellent, Lurch! You've practically solved the murder, except we have a few thousand three-quarter-ton pickups in Blight County. Even little old ladies drive them. But great work."

"Thanks, Boss, but I don't have the slightest idea who the killer might be, if that's important. As you say, we have a few thousand three-quarter-ton pickups in the county."

"I'd look at the pickups on the Fester ranch for starters. What's wrong now?"

"You think Fester's hands will be pleased to see me snooping around their trucks?"

"Good point. They probably haven't lynched anybody out that way in a while, so I better call the foreman and tell him you'll be checking their pickups as a matter of routine. If they give you any trouble, I'll come out and handle it."

"I'll get right on it, Boss. Oh, and here's another thing. The same pickup made two tracks on the skid trail, one from driving in and the other from backing out. Then another truck drove all the way in and backed out, all this about the time Fester was shot. There was another short track from a different vehicle, right at the entrance, like someone had pulled in a short ways and backed out, probably to turn around. The track had been driven over so many times it was impossible to get a cast of it."

"Well, if we do get any leads maybe we can match the other treads. You sure the tracks were made about the same time Fester was shot?"

"Yeah. Pap says the tracks were made during the first snow and the second snow filled them in at the same time it covered the body. That's Pap's idea, anyway. I tell you this, Bo, Pap really knows what he's talking about when it comes to tracks."

"I know he does. And you got some casts of the boot prints."

"Right. But we've got another problem."

"And that is?"

"How did Fester get out to the knoll?"

Tully scratched his jaw while he thought. "He probably drove."

"So what happened to his vehicle? It drive itself back home?"

Tully thought about this. "Good point, Lurch. You work on that one. I have enough problems at the moment."

"What I'm thinking, Boss, one other person had to be there that morning, the one who drove Fester's vehicle away, maybe the same person who drove him out there. Maybe he's the one who did the killing. If not, maybe he saw the killing. He either saw the killing or was supposed to come back later to pick up Fester, in which case he would have seen him dead in the snow with an arrow in his back. If he did, why didn't he report it, unless he was somehow in on the killing?"

"You drive me crazy, Lurch! But you're right. There are at least two people out there who know exactly what happened, the killer and the person who drove Fester's vehicle away."

"One more thing, Boss. You have any idea how I should go about checking the tread on all those pickup tires?"

"Simple. Block some of the tires so the truck won't roll. Then put it in neutral. Borrow a hydraulic jack on rollers. We have one around here someplace. See if you can find it. Jack the truck up so the tire is just off the ground. Give it a spin and look for a tread with that notch in it. If you find a notch that seems to match the notch on the tread on the skid trail, photograph it and make a cast of that part. Finally, chain up the steering wheel of the suspect truck so it can't be driven. Or arrange for it to be hauled into our shop, if you find it."

"Is that all, Boss?"

"Yeah. So you'd better get busy."

Daisy walked over to Lurch's desk, carrying a phone book. "I found three Spokane archery stores in the Yellow Pages, Bo."

"Thanks, Daisy. I'll check them in a moment." Tully patted Lurch on the back. "Good work, young man. Now, when you get a chance, check the tires of all the three-quarter-ton pickups in Blight County. No, only kidding. Start with all the pickups you find at the Fester ranch. Like I said, I'll call the foreman and tell him you're coming out and for the hands not to bother you."

"If you say so, Boss."

"Oh, by the way, Lurch, were you able to find out from the TV weather person the time of the first snowfall at the crime scene?"

"Yeah. Wendy Crooks, the weather girl, pinpointed it exactly for me from her files. It started on December third."

"Might as well give me the times." Tully took out his notebook and pen.

"The snowfall started at four fifty-five in the morning. They were both there at that time, according to the snow in the tracks in the woods and the snow on and under the victim. The victim was shot shortly after the snow started. That's Pap's calculation and I think it's right on the money."

Tully stared at the Unit and shook his head. Then he turned and walked back to his office. Daisy said, "I put the phone book on your desk, with the Yellow Pages open to the archery stores."

"Good. Which is the biggest one?"

"Ed's Archery. They even give archery lessons for both men and women, as well as stock 'the largest supply of archery equipment in the Inland Pacific Northwest,' or so it says in the ad." Daisy had indicated the quotation marks with her fingers.

"Sounds like the kind of place I'm looking for." He went into his office and wrote down the address for Ed's Archery. "I'll be driving to Spokane tomorrow to check on possible evidence."

"And here I thought it would be to pick up your twelve-thousand-dollar check."

Tully smiled. "That, too. I'm glad you mentioned it. But it won't be twelve thousand dollars. My agent takes a hefty chunk out of it for her commission. But right now I have to go over to the medical examiner's office to pick up an arrow. Then I'm headed up to Pine Flats. Get Brian on his cell phone and tell him I'm coming up and for him and Buck to wait for me at the café at noon. We'll have lunch together. I'll stop by the office before I head out."

"Gotcha, Boss."

The next morning, Tully arrived at the office early and unlocked a large metal locker. He took out three bulletproof vests, three 12-gauge pump shotguns, and a bag containing boxes of shotgun shells. As he was carrying this armload down to his Explorer, he met Daisy coming in. She was finishing off the remains of a sandwich. He thought he recognized the aroma.

She frowned at him. "You be careful, Bo. That could be a mean bunch up there at Pine Flats. It produces some of the state's finest criminals."

He grunted at her over his load. "I know. That's why I'm taking Brian and Buck a little extra firepower. Nothing catches a bad guy's attention so much as the sound of a shell being pumped into the firing chamber of a shotgun."

"Just remember that twelve-thousand-dollar check waiting for you in Spokane."

Tully smiled at the thought. "Oh, Daisy, you showed up just in time. I need someone to open my cargo door for me. The key is in my right-hand jacket pocket."

She reached into his pocket and got the key. He followed her down to the sheriff's garage, where she opened the Explorer's luggage hatch for him. He dumped in his load, closed the hatch, then turned and gave her a kiss on the mouth. She gasped. He'd been right, Egg McMuffin.

"I've been wanting to do that for several days," he said, then got in the Explorer and drove off. She stared after him, softly rubbing her lips with the tips of her fingers.

He pulled in next to the medical examiner's office. He got out of the Explorer and tried the door. It was locked. He pushed a button and could hear a buzzer ring inside. He sighed and waited, his hands on his hips. Presently, several slats of the door shade were raised and Willy peeked out. He opened the door and let Tully in.

"I see you're taking more precautions than usual," Tully said.

"Yeah, ever since the ME realized we had a murder victim on our hands, she's insisted the door be kept locked."

"Good idea. Willy, you got any idea if Susan has done any work on the arrow?"

"I should let her tell you about it, but we did do a little research."

Just then Susan stepped through a curtained doorway. "Willy, get back to your job. I will handle all communications with the sheriff."

Willy scooted through a door and disappeared.

"My goodness," Tully said. "You are one stern boss. I'm surprised you have any employees left around here, particularly considering the kind of work you do."

"Well, Willy's all right. He just needs a little nudge now and then to keep him in line, particularly when a nosy sheriff comes snooping around."

Tully laughed. "I wasn't snooping, Susan. In fact, I haven't snooped anything in years. I was investigating. Now could you possibly tell me what you found out about the arrow that killed Fester?"

Susan seemed to think about this for a moment. "I should really give you a written report, but I will tell you a few things now. The arrow definitely killed him. It went through the upper part of his spine, sliced through his lungs and heart, and embedded itself in the back of his breastplate."

"Wow! That's some force!"

Susan nodded. "I'll say it is. We tried to get an estimate of just how much force it would take to go through the spine and embed in the breastplate, so I had Willy go over to the slaughterhouse and pick up some sections of spinal columns from smaller animals and a few organs to duplicate those of Fester. Then we got an arrow similar to the one that killed Fester, the same length and the same arrowhead. Then we fixed up a rack on top of the arrow and placed weights in the rack until the arrow pierced through the vertebrae and organs to the same depth as the arrow in the victim's breastplate."

Tully shook his head. "You people are amazing, Susan. So how much force was behind the arrow when it hit Fester?"

"At least forty pounds."

Tully thought about this. "Does that mean the bow would have had to have a forty-pound pull to it?"

Susan pursed her lips. "I would think at least that. As I recall, you seemed to think the shooter was about twenty yards from the victim. I have no idea how much velocity an arrow shot from a bow with a forty-pound pull would lose over a distance of twenty yards, do you, Bo?"

"Let me think about that. Not the slightest. I am visiting a large archery shop in Spokane tomorrow to find out what information I can about bows and arrows. Do you mind if I take the arrow with me?"

"No, I don't mind. We're done with it. I'll go get it for you."

Tully scratched his jaw. "Uh, Susan, would you mind wrapping it up in a towel and maybe tying some newspapers around it?"

"Yes, we can do that. Has anyone ever told you what a *wuss* you are, Bo?"

"Not when I've been armed."

Chapter 9

Tully got up at five the next morning, ate a breakfast of instant coffee, cornflakes, and milk, and got in his Explorer for the drive to Pine Flats. He had been looking forward to the drive. The road led through a low mountain pass that was still covered with old-growth timber and laced with tumbling streams. Somehow the forest fires and logging early in the century had missed the pass. The road cut between sheer rock cliffs covered with moss. The snow was deeper here and large icicles hung gleaming from the cliffs above. He came to a turn-out and pulled in. Faint blazes on a couple of towering firs marked the trailhead where as youngsters they had once set out on one of their wildest adventures. It had been June 18 nearly thirty years ago. There had been four of them, all in their early teens—Kenny, Vern, Norm, and Bo. They were headed toward a lake high up in the mountain. When they were halfway up the steep winding grade, a late blizzard blew in and caught them wearing nothing but tennis shoes and their summer clothes. Tully had thought they were going to freeze to death, when all at once they came upon a tiny log cabin built by a trapper during the latter half of the last century, when the closest town was nearly a hundred miles away. Tully still remembered a pencil note inscribed on one of the logs—"January 2, 1882, snow 6 feet deep on roof." Tully would like to have seen the cabin again, but a friend of his told him the Forest Service had burned it down. So much for history. He pulled out on the highway and started driving again.

He found Buck and Brian sitting at a table in the ratty little Pine Flats Café. They were studying the menu scrawled on a blackboard on the wall above them. They didn't appear overjoyed.

"What are you two frowning about?" Tully said. "This is the best of fine dining in Pine Flats."

Still looking at the menu, Buck said, "What do you suppose the little hand-scrawled picture of a skull and crossbones after 'Lunch Special' means?"

"It means go with the burger and fries. Everybody knows that."

The waitress came over. She had a dead cigarette stuck to her bottom lip. She held up her pad, ready to write. "What's it going to be, fellas?"

"Three hamburgers, well done," Tully said, sliding in beside Pugh. "And fries."

"Good choice," the waitress said and left, tucking a pencil in a curl of reddish hair above her ear.

"So," Tully said to Pugh. "You guys pick up any leads on our fugitives?"

"Maybe. The Burks claimed they have no idea where Milo and his friends might be hiding out, but the little old lady who lives next door was out getting her newspaper and stopped to talk to us. She turned out to be an eyewitness to the mess at the General Store. She said she knew all about it and said we shouldn't believe a word Clyde Parker says. She saw Milo's two friends go outside and they weren't carrying anything. Milo came up toward the front of the store looking for them and carrying a six-pack of beer under his arm. She said Clyde jumped out from behind a row of shelves and grabbed Milo around the neck in some kind of wrestling hold and started screaming at him that he was trying to steal the beer. Milo has a quick temper. He spun around, jerked loose from Clyde, and punched him in the face, something the old lady said she had wanted to do for years. Knocked Clyde flat on his back on the floor. Then Milo walked out, leaving the six-pack on the floor. She said anything else Clyde might have told us is a lie. He kept screaming he was going to call the cops, and here we are."

Tully sighed. "I'm no fan of Clyde myself. But we've got to find the boys and talk to them at least. Did the lady have any idea where they might be?"

"She said the only place she can think of, they might be hiding in the Burks' summer cabin up on Deer Lake."

"I know Deer Lake," Tully said. "I've fished there a couple of times. She say what side of the lake the cabin is on?"

Pugh thought about this for several seconds. "The east side. She said in summer the sun comes up over the mountains right behind the cabin. It's one of those chalet things."

"I think I know the cabin," Tully said. "What's the lady's name, in case we need to speak to her again?"

"Viola Hilligoss."

"You get her address?"

Pugh pulled a slip of paper from his shirt pocket. "Yeah, 807 Cedar Street."

"I'll stop by and talk to her."

As they started to drive out of Pine Flats, Tully said, "Hold on a minute. I just thought of something. Swing by the sawmill."

An hour later, they stopped on the edge of the road leading past the chalet. The three of them got out of the two cruisers and stood staring at the cabin. Tully said, "Pugh, you got a bullhorn with you?"

"Yeah, Boss."

"Good. Let's pull up in front of the cabin and get out on the side of the vehicle away from it, just as if we expect they might come out shooting."

Buck said, "You think they'll come out shooting, Boss?"

"No, but we'll act as if we do."

"What if Milo and his friends aren't staying in the cabin but somebody else is?"

"Then we'll scare the daylights out of them. That would be awkward but it might exercise their digestive tract." He handed them each a pump shotgun. "Now don't jack your guns until the boys are outside and can hear. The sound of a pump shotgun being loaded has a wonderful calming effect on miscreants."

They drove up the road and coasted to a stop in front of the cabin. The three of them slipped out on the passenger side, Tully pulling along the bullhorn. He aimed the horn at the cabin. "You! In the cabin! This is the police! Come out with your hands above your heads. Make sure your hands are empty!"

No response. Then the door slowly opened and three young men came out, their hands raised high over their heads. Tully thought there was a certain blur around their hands from shaking. He turned to Pugh and Buck and whispered, "Don't pump the guns. It might be too much." He walked around the cruiser and opened a back door. The three young men lowered their hands and climbed in.

"You want me to cuff 'em, Sheriff?" Buck asked.

"Not just yet." Tully slid into the front seat and turned to face the three villains.

"Now here's the deal," he told them. "We're not hauling you off to jail, at least not at this time."

"You're not?" Milo croaked.

"No, there was a witness to what happened at the General Store, and her word is more likely to be trusted than that of Parker."

"Whew!" Milo gasped. "I bet it's Viola, our next-door neighbor."

"Yeah, it is," Tully said. "But I'm not done. I've made certain arrangements down at the sawmill for the three of you."

"You did?" one of the friends asked. "At the sawmill?"

"Yeah, I did. There are three jobs waiting there for you, one on the day shift, one on the night shift, and one on the morning shift. It's the same job for all three of you, pulling off the green chain."

"What's that involve, pulling off the green chain?" Milo asked.

"It's a fun job. By the time you're done with it, you'll think college is the best thing that ever happened to you. By next September, you will be in the greatest shape of your life and will have earned enough money to get you through another two years of college. Higher education works a lot better when you pay for it yourself. You start tomorrow, by the way, so we're dropping you off at your folks', Milo. They're going to be tickled pink to see how all this worked out for you. I'm pretty sure they'll let the three of you live at the chalet. You'll be able to fish off the dock in your spare time, if you feel like it."

"Gee, Bo, this is wonderful," Milo said. "I thought we were done for. Thanks!"

"Thank me after your first shift, Milo. You'll be even more appreciative then."

After they had dropped off the men and were on the way to their motel, Pugh said to Tully, "I heard one time men drop dead pulling off the green chain."

"Oh, sure, but those are old men. Thirty or so. Not strapping young fellows like these three."

Chapter 10

After spending the night at the Pine Flats Motel, Tully drove to Spokane and pulled into a parking lot next to Ed's Archery. The building was huge and was probably owned by an archery expert or somebody who knew at least where an archery expert might be found. A large man approached him as he entered. "May I help you, sir?"

Tully studied him for a moment. The guy definitely looked the type . . . a beard, camo shirt, and jeans. "Sir," Tully said, "I'm Sheriff Bo Tully from Blight County, Idaho, and I need your help in solving a murder."

The clerk's eyes widened. "A murder! Well, I doubt if I can be of much help with that."

Tully explained how Morgan Fester had been killed and showed the clerk the arrow. "Can you tell me anything about this arrow? It was used to kill a man." He held it out to the clerk, who held up his hands and backed away.

"Why don't you just put it over here on the counter," he said. "The light is better."

Tully smiled. "Good idea. I don't like touching the thing myself."

The clerk walked behind the counter, got out a magnifying glass, and ran it along the shaft of the arrow, stopping to study the fletching at some length.

"Anything you can tell me about it?" Tully asked.

"I can tell you this, it isn't a commercial arrow. Somebody made it with hand tools."

"They did?"

"Yeah, the person who used it probably made the arrow himself. Lots of serious archers do that, and we sell them everything they need. The shaft itself looks like it's from stock we sell here at the shop. I suppose it could be bought all over the country, but we're probably the only one to sell it within three hundred miles. The person who made it would have needed a fletching jig, which we also sell here."

"A fletching jig? What's that?" The man pointed to a tool on a shelf. "That's one there."

Tully had seen a similar object once before, in the hobby room of Hillory Fester. "Interesting," he said. "What's it for?"

"It's used to attach the feathers to the shaft."

"Anything else you can tell me about the arrow?"

"Well, yes, it's illegal."

"Illegal? How? Other than it was used to kill a person?"

"Oh sure, there's that," the man said. "Also, the fletching is made from eagle feathers. As I'm sure you know, Sheriff, it's illegal even to possess eagle feathers, let alone use them for fletching."

Tully thought about this for a moment. "I do know that. I guess I just never paid that much attention to the fletching." His head was spinning. A whole new dimension had just opened up in the murder. The shooting may have been a symbolic gesture of some kind, perhaps using part of an eagle to murder a killer of eagles. Who would he be after now? Some kind of mystic nature nut living in a cave back in the mountains? In Blight County that would seriously limit the number of suspects.

"Are you all right?" the clerk asked him. "Could I get you a glass of water?"

"Actually, I could use a glass of water, if it's not too much trouble."

"None at all," the clerk said. "I'll be right back."

He soon returned with a glass of cold water. Tully drank it all down, almost in a single gulp. He shook his head. "Man, I needed that! Well, sir, I much appreciate your help. And your water!"

"No problem, Sheriff. One more thing. As I mentioned, we do sell the same kind of stock that was used to make that arrow shaft. So it's possible its owner was one of our customers. Another thing, it's a rather short arrow, which suggests it was used either by a young archer or by a woman, perhaps a small man."

"Thank you. That could be a big help." Tully pointed to a back wall. "Those big round green things on your back wall, what are those? Targets?"

"Yes, they're made of a very tight fabric that keeps the arrow from penetrating all the way through but holds them firmly. The arrow can easily be removed without its being damaged. They're favored by bow hunters for practice in shooting large objects at greater distances."

Tully nodded. "I don't suppose you keep the names of your customers and what they buy."

"Actually, we do. Oh, we don't keep track of what they buy, but we do have a little catalog we send out a couple times a year to anyone who shops or even visits our store—a list of specials, archery classes, that sort of thing. So we do keep the names and addresses of customers."

Tully couldn't believe his luck. "Sir, would you mind if I checked your list for any addresses in Blight County, Idaho?"

"Well, I shouldn't give you a copy of our list, but to save you the trouble of getting a warrant, I'll make an exception. Would it be all right if we emailed you a list of Idaho customers' names and addresses? People who have made purchases over the past year?"

"Yes, it would. That list might be an enormous help." He gave the clerk the address. "By the way, sir, what's your name, if you don't mind?"

"Ed Simpson. I'm the owner of Ed's Archery."

"Thanks for all your help, Mr. Simpson."

As he was leaving the store, it occurred to Tully where he had seen one of the large green archery targets before: hanging on the side of a barn at the Fester ranch. It hadn't been a wreath at all.

Ah, one more little chore to take care of while in Spokane. He drove around to Jean Runyan's Art Gallery and parked in front. He was pleased to see that the display window was filled with only his paintings, apparently the result of the sale Jean had made the day before. He walked in and was greeted like a conquering hero. Alice, the clerk, ran up and gave him a big hug. Jean walked over smiling. "So, Bo, now you can give up that stupid job and become a full-time painter. You can live on that little farm of yours, grow most of your own food, cut your own firewood, and spend the rest of your time painting."

"Sounds wonderful, Jean. I may just do it. Right now, though, I have a problem—a nasty murder to solve."

"One of these days, Bo, it will be your own murder that needs to be solved and there won't be anyone around to do it."

"Oh, I have many capable people on my staff, Jean. On the other hand, it might take them some time before they quit partying. I run them pretty hard and keep their pay to a minimum, just to save our taxpayers a little money. So, I do believe you have a check for me."

She handed it to him.

"Wow! I'm rich."

"You may notice that I haven't deducted my usual commission."

"I see that."

"I wanted to keep the twelve thousand in one lump sum, so you can make a copy of the check to frame for your studio. I'll take my usual cut out of your next big sale. This will help keep you painting and make us both rich."

"Jean, you are absolutely the best agent I've ever had."

She stood on her tiptoes and gave him a kiss on the cheek. "I'm the *only* agent you've ever had."

As Tully was driving back into Blight City, the radio squawked. It was Florence. "Any available deputy, there's a knife fight at Slade's Bar. Go break it up, before someone gets killed."

Tully clicked on his radio mike. "I'll take care of it, Flo! Call the guys off."

"Be careful, Bo. That's a rough place. Motorcycle gangs hang out there."

"Yeah, yeah."

He double-parked in front of Slade's Bar & Grill, got out, and walked in the door. Two motor-cycle types were circling each other, switchblades thrusting this way and that but no blood in sight. A rough-looking crowd was shouting encouragement, wanting to see blood. Tully walked up and made one wide swing with his bag of shot, laying both combat-ants out cold on the floor. The tavern went silent. He bent over and removed the switchblades from limp hands, folded them shut, and slipped them into one of his pants pockets. He walked over to the bar, the bikers spreading back like a parting of the Red Sea. "Joey, I need a glass of beer. I seem to have worked up a thirst from that bit of exertion." He sat down on a barstool, took out his phone, and called the office. Daisy answered.

"Sweetheart, get a couple of deputies to swing by Slade's and pick up two unconscious bikers, who will probably be conscious by the time the deputies get here. Tell the deputies to put the morons under arrest for assault with intent to kill. But they should first be taken to the hospital and checked for concussions. I don't want to be responsible for killing them, even if they are too stupid to live."

"Got it, Boss."

He clicked off. Joey slid a foaming glass of beer in front of him. A big biker plopped onto a stool next to Tully. "It's always educational to watch you work, Bo."

Tully turned to him and smiled. "You think maybe I should charge tuition, Mitch?"

"I know a lot of folks here who could profit from the class."

Tully called to the bartender. "Joey, give my friend here a beer. Put it on my tab."

"You don't have a tab, Bo, but the beers are on the house." Joey drew a beer and shoved it in front of Mitch.

The biker took a sip. "Working on any interesting crimes these days, Bo?"

"Naw, just the usual. Got a murder out on South River Road that's kind of interesting."

"Oh yeah, I heard about Ole Fester. He was a piece of work. You got any idea who done him?"

"No. You heard anything, Mitch?"

"Not really. He messed around with some of the women who hang out here at Slade's. Their boyfriends and husbands might be good candidates, although I'm not sure why. If I hear anything of interest, I'll pass it along to you."

"I'd appreciate hearing anything you turn up."

A siren wailed faintly in the distance. "I've got to hit the road, Mitch. Look after the two morons and my deputies while they're here, okay?"

"You got it, Bo."

Chapter 11

The next morning, having picked up his daily break-fast of Egg McMuffin at McDonald's and munched it on his way into the office, Tully parked in his reserved space behind the courthouse and got out, brushing the breakfast crumbs from his jacket.

He walked into the briefing room, the heels of his boots *klocking* nicely on the marble-chip floor. The place was empty, except for Daisy. She gave him a smile. "You've been busy, Boss."

"Yep, one thing after another."

"You pick up your check?"

He smiled. "Are you kidding me? I wouldn't leave it with my agent for another minute. Actually, she was very generous. She didn't take out her share. So I'll make a copy of the check, frame it, and hang it on my wall, just as a reminder."

"Of what?"

"Beats the heck out of me. I've never in my whole life seen this much money in one place, at least not money that belongs to me." He looked into his office. Lurch was sitting in his chair, his feet up on Tully's desk, reading what was probably Tully's newspaper.

"I see the Unit is as busy as ever."

"Yeah," Daisy said. "Lurch is working his finger to the bone."

"Just one finger?"

"You don't want him to exhaust himself, do you, Boss?"

"I guess not." Tully strode into his office.

Lurch's feet hit the floor and he leaped up. "Geez, Boss, you took me by surprise. I didn't expect you in before noon."

"Couldn't sleep. So what have you come up with?"

"Just what I told you, the tracks in the woods."

"Okay, here's what I want you to do now. Call all the airlines and find out which one Hillory Fester flew out on. If they won't give you the information over the phone, ask them to fax the information to Blight County Sheriff Bo Tully at the office fax number. If they won't give us the information at all, call the FBI in Boise and ask the feds to get it for us."

An hour later Lurch knocked on his door. Tully waved him in. "What did you find out?"

"The clerks I talked to said they would have to get permission from their bosses to release any information about passengers. So I asked them if they could release information on persons who weren't passengers. They did some checking and said they had no information that a Hillory Fester had ever been a passenger."

"All airlines?"

"All in the region."

"That's weird."

The Unit said, "Yeah, I thought so, Boss. Maybe she's still here."

"No, she's not. I called and talked to her in Mexico. Anyway, don't forget to take that cast you made of the truck track in the woods and see if it matches any of the pickups at the Fester ranch. Talk to Sheridan first. Then I don't think anyone will give you any trouble."

"Should I wear my gun, Boss?"

"No!"

Chapter 12

The following morning Tully pulled into the parking lot of the Silver Tip Hotel. He rang the doorbell and Ed answered. "Bo, back so soon?" He held the door for Tully.

"Yeah, Ed. I'd like to talk to your chef, if she's not busy."

"I think the ladies are all finished with breakfast, Bo. I'll see if I can hunt Sasha down for you. Man the door for a bit while I go look for her."

Tully had no more flopped into a chair than the doorbell rang. He got up and answered it. Three young fellows stood there looking up at him. He guessed them for college students, probably freshmen.

"May I help you, gentlemen?" he said.

"Well, yeah," said the fellow who was probably the leader of the group. He must have been older and more experienced, possibly a sophomore. "We heard about the Silver Tip and thought we'd stop by and check it out."

Tully stroked his mustache and nodded thoughtfully. "I see. Well, I don't see a problem with that, gentlemen. I will, of course, have to check your IDs, to make sure you are twenty-one or older."

"How come?" asked the apparent leader of the group.

"Well, in case one of you isn't twenty-one and he drops dead on the premises, as often happens with some of our more extreme treatments, I would be able to notify the next of kin."

"Geez!" one of the younger ones said. "If I dropped dead here, I certainly wouldn't want my parents notified. Let's go!" They hurried out the door.

Ed came out and looked around. "I thought we had some customers. What happened to them?"

"One of them just remembered an important appointment. You find Sasha?"

"Yeah, she said she'd meet you in the dining room in a few minutes. Go on in, Bo."

Tully walked into the dining room and sat down at a table. One of the ladies came over with a tray containing a pot of coffee, two cups, sugar, cream, and two cinnamon rolls. "Hope you like cinnamon rolls, Sheriff. They're hot out of the oven. Sasha said to tell you she will be right out."

"Great! Thank you very much. The cinnamon rolls smell wonderful."

The lady gave him a big smile and left. Sasha soon came rushing out of the kitchen, wiping her hands on a towel.

"Hi, Bo. Sorry to keep you waiting. I had some stuff to finish up."

"No problem. I just had a few questions to ask you. When you were hunting, did you use a bow or a rifle?" He pinched off a piece of a cinnamon roll and popped it in his mouth. Delicious!

"A rifle. Why?"

"Let me ask the questions, Sasha. What caliber of rifle?"

"A twenty-five twenty."

"That's awfully light for hunting."

She smiled. "Not if you know what you're doing, Sheriff."

Tully smiled back and nodded. "You must have been a pretty good shot."

"Always aimed for the head. One time when I was fourteen I was out deer hunting by myself. Didn't see any, but walking back home along Sand Creek, I saw this flock of birds fly into a little leafless tree ahead of me. I didn't know what kind they were. They looked like grouse, except smaller, but I knew grouse didn't go around in flocks. They looked good to eat, though. I took aim at the lowest one on the tree so that when I shot he wouldn't fall through the rest and disturb them. I then worked my way up the tree, picking them off one by one. After I'd killed about half the flock, the others caught on to what was happening and took off. I can tell you, Sheriff, those birds were tremendous eating! My family loved them, but it was years before I figured out what kind they were."

"And they were?"

"Huns! Hungarian partridges."

"No wonder you didn't know what they were. Huns are very rare around this neck of the woods. They were probably some experiment the Fish and Game Department was trying out, to get Huns established in this area. Maybe you wiped out half the project for them."

"Well, they were delicious, anyway. So why did you want to know if I ever hunted with a bow?"

"Just cleaning up a few details in my investigation. I know you have a keen interest in birds, despite murdering all the Huns in Blight County. Strange to come across a flock of them around here."

"Yeah. Speaking of strange, have you ever seen a big circle drawn in fresh snow with no tracks leading to or away from it?"

Tully frowned as if to search his memory. "No, can't say I ever have."

"Well, I have!"

"Really?"

"Yes, it was in a small field next to a woods not far from here. But there was a nasty barbwire fence between me and it, so I couldn't get near enough to see what might have made it. There were no tracks leading to or away from it. Do you have any idea what could have made such a thing?"

"Maybe a flying saucer?"

"Be serious!"

"I am. What else could have made it?"

Sasha said, "I don't know. But I think it must have been a sign meant to tell us something. Shoot, maybe it *was* made by a flying saucer."

Tully was silent for a moment. He chose not to tell Sasha about his own close encounter with the silvery disk or his circle in the snow, either. "That would be my guess. You have any idea?"

"No. Maybe it was made by birds to tell us something?"

"You think a bird is smart enough to communicate with us?"

"Not just one bird but maybe a whole flock?"

"A whole flock?"

"Yeah! Suppose a whole flock of a hundred eagles, say, is perched together in a woods. Think of each of them as a single cell in one large organism, the flock, which has a single intelligence spreading through it. Each eagle is tuned in to the same flock mind. Maybe one of them is told to fly over and make the sign."

Tully smiled. "I'm having a little trouble with this theory, that a flock of birds could have a single intelligence. You are telling me the circle was quite large and appeared to have been drawn in the snow with a giant protractor? Suppose that a flock of eagles is that smart, where would it get a giant protractor? Do you actually think a flock of birds is that smart, Sasha?"

Sasha frowned. "Bo, have you ever seen a big flock of starlings in the fall, getting ready to fly south, maybe a thousand birds all together? Suddenly they take off and form a wide flat ribbon of birds in the air, and that ribbon ripples and turns this way and that, then rises straight up in the air, plummets back toward the ground, spreads out, and makes a huge wave?"

Tully nodded. "As a matter of fact, I have, Sasha. I've seen starlings do just that sort of thing in the fall, getting ready to fly south. It was out near Moses Lake, in the wheatlands of Washington State. Saw it three years ago, driving to Seattle."

Sasha seemed to sigh in relief. "Well, okay then. How do you suppose each of those little birds knows what to do for his tiny part in the performance?"

"I haven't a clue. As a matter of fact, I've wondered about that myself, although not for very long."

"Do you think maybe the head bird says to the bird next to him, 'First we're going to take off, make ourselves into a big flat ribbon, twist and turn and make a big loop, shoot straight up into the air, then dive down and make a huge rolling wave. Pass it along!'"

Tully burst out laughing. He shook his head and said, "No, I don't think it happens like that. But I don't have a clue how they manage it. Do you, Sasha?"

"Yeah."

"I was afraid you would."

She smiled. "It's like I said. I think maybe when all the individual birds gather into a large flock, the flock becomes a single organism, each of the birds a single cell in the organism. And they share an overall intelligence."

Tully took a sip of his coffee and popped the last piece of cinnamon roll into his mouth. "Well, I can't say you've convinced me, but you've certainly made me think. I have to leave now. You've given me a headache, and I have a hard day tomorrow. Oh, by the way, what kind of vehicle do you drive when you're running around in the woods looking for birds and stuff?"

"A pickup. Why?"

"No particular reason. A three-quarter-ton four-wheel-drive, by any chance?"

"Yeah. Is there any other kind?"

"Apparently not in Blight County. Anyway, the Sheriff's Department is running a little study. Would you mind if a deputy in my department came by and checked your tires? He's making a study of Blight County three-quarter-ton pickup truck tires and we might as well get you eliminated from our investigation."

"I bet this has something to do with your investigation of Morg Fester's murder, doesn't it?"

Tully tried to think of a lie but none came to mind. "Yeah, it does."

Sasha was quiet for a moment, apparently thinking the request through. After a bit she said, "There were times if I ever caught Morg killing eagles, I would have shot him. But sure, my pickup truck is the blue Ford out in the employees' parking lot." She gave him her license number.

"Thanks, Sasha. I hated to ask. Just part of my job."

"I know, Bo. Don't worry about it."

Chapter 13

"**P**ull harder on that left oar, Pap!" Tully shouted at the old man. "Try to bring us into that slack water between the knoll and the island. Now! Row harder! Otherwise, we're gonna miss the island altogether!"

Pap yelled back. "If you know so much about rowing a drift boat, Bo, mebby you should crawl back here and do it!"

"Can't, Pap! One of us has to stay here in the bow and be captain, to figure out how to get where we're going! So follow my directions!"

The old man muttered something under his breath and pulled back hard on the oar.

"Pull harder, Pap! We're missing the island!"

Tully stood up and stared off toward the middle of the island as they swept on by. "I can't even see the circle from here!"

"Mebby you'll have to float over it in a balloon, because I ain't fighting this current in a drift boat again!"

"Try to make it back to shore! Otherwise we'll have to shoot the Narrows and take out down at Henry's Landing! You ever shoot those rapids?"

"Only in my worst nightmares! Never occurred to me I'd ever be stupid enough to shoot them when I was awake!"

Minutes later they were swept into the mouth of the Narrows. Halfway through they climbed a wall of water so steep the drift boat kept slipping back down. Tully stretched out over the bow as far as he could and jammed an oar down into the boiling current. Instantly they were pulled over the crest and plunged into a deep, dark, watery hole. The roaring was so intense both Tully and Pap were hoarse for days afterward. When they finally popped out of the Narrows, Pap somehow managed to maneuver the drift boat onto the takeout ramp at Henry's Landing. Then he called his girlfriend on his cell phone, asking her to drive over to the river, retrieve his truck and boat trailer, and bring them down to Henry's Landing.

Tully asked, "You recovered yet from the Narrows, Pap?"

The old man seemed to turn the question over in his mind. "All I can say, Bo, those rapids would make a fine cure for constipation."

"Worked for me," Tully said.

Pap stared at him. "You better be kidding. Otherwise, you ain't ridin' back in my truck."

"Yeah, I'm kidding. But just barely."

Back at Pap's place, Tully got into his Explorer and drove to the office. The whole staff seemed busy, even Herb Eliot, his undersheriff, whose chief talent was avoiding work and anything that might put him in the way of it. Daisy was typing up a form of some kind, and Lurch was hunched over his computer. Tully looked around and said, "So you all heard me coming down the hallway. One of these days I'm going to switch from boots to shoes and catch you in your normal state of fun and games."

"No way, Boss," Daisy said. "We were all buried in work, just like always."

"Ha!" Tully said. "Lurch, get your butt over to my office. I want to know what you've found out about our murder."

Lurch strolled over, shut the office door behind him, and flopped into a chair. "You catching a cold, Boss? You sound hoarse."

Tully stared at him. "No. Just the strain of the job. So what have you found out about Fester's murder?"

"The same thing I told you up at the crime scene. The pickup tracks on the skid trail showed that one vehicle had driven in a short ways and then backed out. The tracks indicated it was a three-quarter-ton and probably a four-wheel-drive, which is what most pickups that size are around here. Its tread didn't match the other treads on the skid trail. I think it must have just been turning around. The snow in the other tire tracks, the ones that went in thirty yards or so, indicates they were made the same time as the new snow started, when Fester was shot. It was Pap who pointed that out to me. I found size-six or maybe size-eight boot tracks in the woods that appear to have been made at the same time the victim was killed. I got a good cast of one of those, and if we ever find a pair of boots belonging to a suspect, we might get a match. Finally, I checked the pickup trucks at the Fester ranch and the one at Silver Tip you wanted me to check and didn't get a match."

Tully leaned forward and rested his arms on the desk. "I'm glad to hear that about Silver Tip. I was worried Sasha might somehow be involved in this, mostly because of her fascination with birds, eagles in particular. Fester used to tease her about how he loved killing eagles. So you didn't find any treads on the pickups at Fester's ranch that matched the tracks on the skid trail?"

"Nothing. I checked every pickup there, and Jeff Sheridan said all the hands were at the ranch at the time and so were their pickups. He could have been lying, of course. He was flying down to the ranch in Mexico the next day."

"Really? Maybe he's meeting up with Hillory Fester, who should be flying back for the funeral. Who's in charge up here?"

"A young guy by the name of Wiggens. We may have trouble with him, if we need to check the ranch for anything more. Oh, he did tell me one pickup from the ranch was missing. He said Mrs. Fester probably drove it to Cabo. I don't know why he told me that but he did. Anyway, that would explain why there's no airline record of a Mrs. Fester having flown down there by plane."

"Wiggens!" Tully said. "You leave him to me, Lurch. How about the pickups owned by the ranch?"

"Jeff said they all were there, including the rig Fester drove."

Tully sighed and leaned back in his chair. "So where does that leave us now, as to who shot Morg?"

Lurch shook his head. "I don't know. I measured the distance from where the tracks out of the woods stopped to where we found Fester's body. It was almost exactly twenty yards. I figure an arrow traveling that far wouldn't lose much force before hitting the target. So it seems to me we would be looking for a bow with at least a forty-pound pull."

"Pretty good, Lurch. That's about what I figured."

Chapter 14

Daisy walked into his office and sat down across the desk from him. She was studying her stenography pad. "You want to hear what's been going on here at the sheriff's office, Bo?"

"Not really. But shoot."

"You got a call from your fortune-teller. She says it's very important that you see her as soon as possible. Apparently your life is in danger again."

So Etta was back in town. Etta Gorsich was very attractive, except for being a fortune-teller and a few years older than Tully. "She mention any particulars about my life being in danger?"

"No, I think she was withholding those in the hope of getting you over to that creepy place of hers as soon as possible."

"You have to remember, Daisy, that Etta has always been right-on in the past about persons intent on killing me."

"Bo, you always have persons intent on killing you. I could predict that, and I'm not even a psychic."

"I know, but some persons are more intent on killing me than others. I'll drop in on her after lunch. Speaking of lunch, how would you like to grab a bite over at Crabbs?"

"Sounds like fun. Can we drink?"

"Only a glass of wine each. We'll be working, you know."

"Aren't we always."

"There's something I've been meaning to ask you, but I keep forgetting what it is."

"You probably want the rap sheet on some criminal."

"Maybe," Tully said. "Oh, I know something. Get me Hank Schmitt on the phone. He's the boss up at Pine Flats sawmill."

"You know the number?"

"No. I'll look it up. I haven't needed a board in years."

Daisy went back to her desk, shutting his door a little louder than necessary, he thought. That's what he got for being too friendly with the help, not to mention having had an affair with this one in particular. Bad! Bad! He picked up his phone and dialed a number. A woman answered.

"Hi, Etta. It's Bo. I was tickled pink to hear you're back in town."

"Oh, Bo, it's so good to hear your voice! As usual, I've been sensing some sort of violence hovering around you."

"You know that's part of my job, sweetheart. Don't pay any attention to it. I'll swing by after work. Seems as if you've been gone practically forever this time."

"That's so nice of you to say, Bo. It's only been a couple of months. I have to make a living, you know."

"I'm pretty sure you're independently wealthy by now, Etta, with all those giants of industry you have as clients back east."

"Oh, they're not giants by any measure, Bo. They're simply older little boys and girls in need of some psychic reinforcement. Some of the boys are gray and bald and a bit overweight, but they still need someone to lean on from time to time."

"How about the little girls?"

"They're all trim and fit and pretty and a bit flinty about the eyes. I can soften them up, though. Everybody needs somebody, and I try to be that somebody."

"I'm sure they need all the help you give them, Etta. As a matter of fact, I could use a little of that myself."

Daisy stuck her head in the door. "As soon as you're done with your fortune-teller, Hank Schmitt is on line two."

He nodded at her, then said into the phone, "Got to run, Etta. Crime waits for no one."

"Just be careful, Bo."

"I will." Even though he didn't believe in fortune-telling, Etta had a way of setting his nerves on edge. He punched line two.

"Hank, thanks for getting back to me. I just wanted to check on our three young criminals."

"They're doing great, Bo. Oh, their first few days on the green chain, I wasn't sure they were going to make it, but they hung in there. Now they're hardening up muscles they never knew they had."

"Great, Hank. I've been worried about them. Men have dropped dead pulling off the green chain."

"Yeah, after the boys showed up for work the first few days we had to check them for signs of life ever so often, but now they're settling in and working hard. It doesn't hurt that I'm paying them twenty dollars an hour, either. I don't think one of them has ever had this much money before, money he earned himself, and they're too tired at the end of the day to go out and spend any of it. As a matter of fact, I don't think they'll ever spend it. They've worked too hard for every dime. If you have any more criminals you'd like to send my way, Bo, I'd appreciate it, as long as they're under the age of thirty."

Tully laughed. "Well, just so the three criminals hold out through the spring and summer, I'll look for some additional green-chain folks for you. I'd like to get all three of these back to college in the fall."

Schmitt said, "After pulling off the green chain, Bo, everything in life is up from there. I'm sure they'll love college as never before."

"Hank, the next time I turn up any young healthy criminals I will definitely send them your way."

Chapter 15

Lester Cline, the headwaiter at Crabbs, broke into a beaming smile at the sight of Tully and Daisy walking through the restaurant's front door. One of his aims in life seemed to be getting Bo and Daisy married. He swept two menus off the counter and rushed them over. "Oh, what a pleasure to see you two together once again. I'll show you to your special table. I keep it reserved just for the two of you."

"Thanks, Lester, but this is strictly a business luncheon. It's Daisy's turn and she's paying."

Daisy said, "It is not my turn, Lester, and I'm not paying. We're here for a business lunch, as Bo says, so the county is paying."

"Even better. The tip is always really good when the county pays." He showed them to their table and spread a large linen napkin on each of their laps.

"What's the special today?" Tully asked.

"You know what the special is today, Bo. It's what the special is every day at Crabbs for lunch."

"In that case, I'll take the special. It's always good."

Daisy said, "I'll take the special, too, Lester. And two glasses of wine. White zinfandel, if you please. I don't know if Bo wants any."

"That's okay, Lester. I'll just drink one of hers."

Lester looked confused.

Daisy laughed. "Don't worry about it, Lester. I'll give one of mine to Bo."

The waiter wandered off, rather aimlessly, Tully thought. Daisy could be an extremely confusing person when she was in the mood. He had long ago given up trying to understand her moments of whimsy.

Daisy said, "Hard to believe you once sent Lester up for five years. What was that for again?"

"Boosting cars. He only did three, though—years, not cars. Got out on good behavior."

"And gave up on a life of crime?"

"As far as we know, Daisy. Can't say the same for the chef here at Crabbs."

"What! I didn't know he had a criminal history!"

"You eat here and can say that!"

"Bo, it isn't that bad. Hush, here comes Lester."

Lester came mincing up, a white linen napkin over his arm, two glasses of white wine and the remainder in a bottle on the tray. He served them with elaborate gestures, something that caused Tully to think of a French waiter, even though he hadn't actually been to France.

"Lovely, Lester," Daisy said, while Tully frowned up at him.

"Thank you, Daisy. It's so nice to hear words of appreciation from time to time." He rolled his eyes in Tully's direction. "So is it the lunch special for both of you, or are you going to try your luck?"

"Let me think, Lester," Tully said. "Hmm. I think we'll both have the lunch special."

"Very good choice, sir. It hasn't produced any fatalities in over a week." He minced back toward the kitchen. Tully guessed it was an act. Lester really wasn't the mincing type.

He sipped his wine. "Not bad."

Daisy frowned at him. "Bo, you know the wine here is always good. Anyway, while Lester is gone, what do you think about us getting back together? I've dated a couple of guys since we broke up, and I have to tell you, the pickings are very thin out there when it comes to men."

"Daisy, this is Blight City in the middle of Blight County. I take it you've never read 'The Cave.'"

"'The Cave'? No, I can't say I have."

"That's because it was written by Socrates, who was a bit before your time. Also because Socrates never wrote anything. All he did was talk. Plato wrote down what he said, and that's how we know about 'The Cave.'"

"I hate philosophy, Bo."

"I hate it, too, and would never have read Plato if it hadn't been forced on me by a professor in college. The guy was a monster. Take another shot of wine, because you're going to need it."

"Oh, no! Please don't tell me about 'The Cave' when I'm about to have lunch."

"I'll just give you the gist of my version. You see, there was this band of people who were born into a cave and lived their whole lives there. The master of the cave—I forget what he was called—somehow projected images up on the wall, perhaps with a stone projector of some kind, and those images were all the cave people knew about the world outside the cave, if there was a world out there. So here's my point. I think Socrates meant that if people never leave the tiny culture of people they are born into, that is all they know of the world. They may get images on the wall from outside, like in newspapers and magazines and television and movies nowadays, but they never have firsthand knowledge of it. Are you following me, Daisy? I'm working on your education here."

Daisy took a swig of her wine. "Yeah, I think I'm following you, Bo."

"My point is, if you date someone who was born in Blight, raised in Blight, and lived his whole life in Blight, he will be a Blighter. His whole world is Blight, except for the images on the wall of the cave or, in the Blighter's case, maybe television or the movies."

"Okay, I get your point. I think maybe Socrates was right. My question to you is, since you escaped the cave of Blight, why did you come crawling back into it?"

Tully frowned. "Good question. 'Crawling' seems a bit extreme, but I guess it was because I understood Blight. I feel more comfortable with what I understand, bad as it might be, than with what I don't. I can talk hunting and fishing and chain saws and double-bitted axes and huckleberries with the best of the Blighters."

Daisy stared off into the distance. "Well, I went to secretarial college for one year and came back to Blight, too. I still can't talk hunting or fishing or chain saws. Blight does grow on you, though. Or you on it. Oh, here comes Lester."

The waiter arrived with two large bowls of salad, each heaped with chunks of dark meat. "Grilled-steak salad!" he said, placing the salads in front of them.

"Lester!" Daisy exclaimed. "It smells delicious!"

"I must admit that it is."

Tully stared at his salad. "Crabbs must be coming up in the world."

Lester smiled. "It's not a hard climb, Bo, when you're already the finest restaurant in all of Blight City."

After the waiter left, Daisy said, "Once again, you have managed to avoid answering my question."

"What question is that, Daisy?"

"I asked you what you thought about us getting back together again. I know that a while back you and Jan Whittle went off to dinner in the Seattle Space Needle, a two-day trip, as I recall. I assume that was the reason she and Darrel got divorced."

"I don't think so, Daisy. The reason for the divorce is that Darrel is a turnip. The reason for our little trip, Jan was just paying off a debt, mainly for my risking my life to trudge up into the mountains to find that miserable runaway kid Glen Cliff for her. I can assure you nothing of consequence happened on the Space Needle trip, but Jan told me she and Darrel already planned to divorce. Our little trip, Jan's and mine, was just like when we were boyfriend and girlfriend back in grade school. Nothing of consequence ever happened back then, either. As I recall, we never even spoke. That's the way grade-school romances went back then."

"Did you speak on your Seattle trip?"

"Just what I told you. But Jan has no interest in getting married or even having a serious relationship again. She makes a good living as principal of the grade school and loves the work. And she wants to enjoy her freedom from the turnip. But to answer your question, yes, I've been thinking a great deal about you and me getting back together again. Jan and I even talked about that. So there."

"Really? You talked about us getting together again?"

"Well, yeah. I didn't want her to get any ideas while she was out there overnight with someone like me."

Daisy burst out laughing.

Tully frowned but went on. "I have been thinking how nice it would be if someone got up on ice-cold mornings and built my fire, so I could get up to a warm house."

Daisy smiled. "Maybe you should take in a boarder. Oh, by the way, Leroy Fagan called while you were out investigating your murder."

"So what does our district attorney want with me now?"

"He didn't say. But I got the impression it was something involving Blight County judges. He mentioned something about the FBI and said he wanted to talk to you as soon as you had the chance."

Tully forked a piece of grilled steak into his mouth and chewed it thoughtfully. "Do you suppose somebody thinks Blight County judges might get paid off by trial attorneys simply wanting to win cases? What is the world coming to? Judges have to eat, too."

"Our county judges get paid exceedingly well, I think. Fagan didn't say why he wanted to talk to you, but that would be my guess. He just happened to mention the FBI."

"Paying off judges is an age-old tradition in Blight County," Tully said. "I can't imagine why Fagan or the FBI would get excited about that now. Are they going to let cases be decided by law? Now that is something really scary. There go a few more of our beloved traditions."

Tully ate another piece of his steak. It was surprisingly good. Something was going on behind the scenes at Crabbs. Then he said, "So Leroy is bothered by payoffs to judges? Maybe he hasn't been getting his cut. I'm not sure I want to get involved in our judges' haggling over their payoffs. Not that I would suspect them of such a thing. Haggling, I mean."

"Well, the FBI apparently does. They've sent an agent up to check into the complaints."

"Not . . . ?"

Yes, Angie Phelps. She's in charge of the whole northern part of Idaho now."

"Just my luck!"

"Right. Nothing you hate worse than having to work with a smart, pretty, shapely female FBI agent."

Tully rubbed his jaw and thought about the pretty agent. They had worked several crimes together.

Daisy glared at him. "Stop thinking about Angie, Bo."

Chapter 16

Tully clumped up the long steep flight of wooden
steps to Etta Gorsich's house, an old, gray, creepy-
looking structure perfectly suited to a fortune-teller.
It was perched on a hill overlooking Blight City. He
never paid much attention to Etta's warnings, but several of them had proved to be right-on. If he counted
all the warnings Etta had come up with, he figured she
had guessed correctly on a couple of them. Fortune-
tellers apparently worked on percentages. He glanced
up. Etta was standing on her porch watching him. He
gave her a weak little wave. The steps seemed greater
in number than usual. He stopped and rested, turning to gaze out over the city, as if he had just thought
of something he had better observe there. Etta called
down to him.

"Bo, I've told you before, you're getting much too
old to be sheriff of a place like Blight County!"

"Just enjoying the view, Etta!"

He plodded on up the steps. Etta spread her arms for him and he stepped into them, giving her a squeeze to keep from collapsing.

"Oh, Bo, it's so good to see you. Come on in. I have a pot of tea ready." She opened the door and he stepped into the sumptuous living room: polished hardwood tables, pink silk covering a large plump sofa with matching chairs, large windows overlooking the forestlands to the west, a silver tea set resting on a coffee table in front of the sofa. Apparently, the fortune-telling business was a bit more than lucrative, even in an economically depressed area like Blight County. The room always came as a bit of a shock to Tully, particularly after having experienced the exterior of the home.

He walked over, eased himself down on the sofa, and slid in behind the coffee table. "So, Etta, what's this dire warning you have to give me?"

She sat down in a chair across from him and poured the tea. "Two spoonfuls of sugar, as I recall."

Tully nodded. Etta never forgot anything. She had the finest mind of anyone he knew and had no reason for the pretense of being a fortune-teller. Her advice to business tycoons came from her intellect and knowledge of the markets. Fortune-telling was only a cover, because tycoons couldn't believe a woman could possibly be as smart as Etta.

Tully sipped his tea. Perfect, as always. "So what's this threat I'm supposed to be so concerned about?"

She frowned. "You know somebody named Fletch, don't you?"

"Fletch! How do you know about Fletch? He's locked up in prison. Been there for the past five years. Be another five before he has a chance to get out. His real name isn't Fletch, anyway. It's George Mahoney. The gang he ran with just called him Fletch."

"Oh," Etta said. "I didn't know he was in prison. My sources just told me he made a serious threat against you and for you to be wary."

Tully smiled. "Etta, it will be so long before Mahoney gets out of prison, I get this ridiculous dream of him and me. He's chasing me down the street, both of us shooting at each other and we're both in wheelchairs."

Etta looked puzzled. "My source didn't mention prison, Bo. I'm sorry. I certainly wouldn't want to worry you for no reason."

"Not a problem. I'm sure your sources meant well and tell them I appreciate their concern. No doubt Fletch has been saying quite a few mean things about me."

They chatted and sipped tea for a few minutes and then Etta said, "Do you think you and I could at long last make that trip up through Idaho we've talked about for years? It's such a beautiful state and I would love to see the rest of it."

Tully took a sip of tea while he thought about this. "Etta, beginning in June, I have a month off. If you can make it then, I'm all for it. I may have to check with Daisy first, though."

"Your secretary? Why on earth would you have to check with your secretary?"

"Daisy keeps track of what I have to do. If she didn't, I'd have to, and I already have too much work."

"I guess it's a good thing you have Daisy, then. You have more than enough work, Bo. Sometimes you look exhausted."

Tully laughed. "I fake that, Etta. It gets me a lot of sympathy. Well, actually, it doesn't get me any sympathy, but I keep hoping it might. Anyway, thanks for telling me about Fletch. I'm sure he takes my name in vain and makes threats of all kinds while he's doing his time. Your informants are probably just picking up on that."

"I hope so, Bo."

Tully sipped the last of his tea and stood up. "I'm sorry to sip and run, Etta, but I've got to get back to the office. Crime waits for no one."

"I'm sure it doesn't, Bo. Just be careful."

Chapter 17

By the time Tully got back to the office, the night shift was arriving—eight deputies, the night supervisor, and the jail staff. Daisy was clearing her desk. "Oh, Bo! I didn't expect you back. How was your fortune-teller?"

"Etta was fine, thank you. Beautiful as ever, very smart, and intensely interested in me."

Daisy smiled. "Too bad she's over sixty years old."

"Oh yeah, there's that. So anything of interest going on here?"

"I'm afraid so. We got an alert from the state police. George Mahoney faked a heart attack, managed to slip out of the prison hospital unit, and made his escape."

Tully could feel the hairs on the back of his neck rise.

"Gee, Bo," Daisy said. "I didn't mean to shock you."

"It wasn't you, Daisy, and it wasn't George Mahoney. So Fletch is on the loose. I'd better swing by Slade's on my way home and have a talk with what remains of his old gang, if they're still hanging out there."

Daisy put on her coat and grabbed her purse. "Speaking of Slade's, your two knife fighters got a clean bill of health from the hospital. No concussions from accidental contact with your blackjack."

"Good. I didn't mean to hit them as hard as I did. It wasn't a blackjack, anyway. Just a bag of lead shot I use for loading my own shotgun shells. Maybe for the moment I was simply overcome by their monumental stupidity and went a little berserk. So what's their status now?"

"They're both in separate cells downstairs, whining to be released."

Tully thought about this. "I'm the one who made up the charges against them, assault with intent to kill. Why else get into a knife fight? Oh, right, stupidity. But if stupidity were a crime, we would have half of Blight County in jail. I'll drop down and have a talk with the boys before I head out, and maybe I'll see if the judge will drop the charges. What are their names, anyway?"

Daisy checked a folder on her desk. Felix Burdock and Milton Fry.

"What?" Tully said. "Give me their names again."

Daisy did. "Felix and Milton."

Tully sighed. "Men by the names of Felix and Milton don't get into knife fights. Are you sure those are their real names?"

Daisy said, "Bo, these days I'm not sure of anything. I imagine the arresting officers checked the ID in their wallets, if they had any."

Daisy left and Tully walked over to the elevator, enjoying as always the sound his three-thousand-dollar boots made on the marble-chip floor. *So few pleasures in life,* he thought, *you have to appreciate any that happen along.* He got out of the creaky old elevator on the basement floor, which housed the jail. Lulu, the elderly jail matron, was on duty behind her desk. A steel-barred door and a double row of cells stretched down a corridor behind her.

"Good evening, Lulu," he said, greeting the stout little lady. Her gray hair was tied in its usual bun.

"Bo, how nice to see you! What brings you down to the dungeon this time of day?"

"Oh, I just felt like having a chat with two of your inmates, Felix and Milton."

Lulu laughed. "Aren't those the two most awful names you ever heard for jailbirds?"

"They are indeed, Lulu. I heard you had the good sense to put each in a cell by himself. A cellmate would have felt obligated just out of self-respect to beat up a person named Milton or Felix. Those names are usually reserved for dentists and librarians. Can you believe these two characters were arrested for a knife fight?"

"It's hard to imagine, Bo. I understand you coldcocked both of them with a single stroke of your blackjack."

"Yes, I did, but that was without knowing their names. I was simply responding to the monumental stupidity of two persons engaging in a knife fight in this day and age. Since they are regulars at Slade's Bar & Grill, however, I've been thinking they might have some useful information for me. Where's your assistant hiding out, anyway?"

She pointed to a door at the end of the room. "Oh, Bert disappeared into our restroom about an hour ago. He probably fell asleep in there. You can either flush him out yourself, Bo, or just flush him, makes no difference to me."

Tully thought about this for a moment. "I'd better let you flush him out, Lulu."

She put her hands to her mouth and shouted, "Get your business done in there fast as you can, Bert, and get that butt out here! Sheriff Tully is after you!"

The tall, skinny Bert burst through a door at the end of the room and came scurrying over. "A man don't get a moment's peace around this joint, Sheriff."

Tully scratched his chin to keep from smiling. "Sorry to disturb you, Bert, but I need you to put Burdock in the interrogation room. I want to have a little chat with him."

"You want him cuffed, Bo?"

"Bert, his name is Felix."

"Oh yeah, I forgot for a second. Hope I didn't offend you, Sheriff."

"No offense taken."

A few minutes later, Bert had Felix in the tiny interrogation room. Tully opened the door, stepped in, and closed the door behind him. He sat down at a small table. Felix peered back at him from the other side. He was a large man but soft in appearance, with dull eyes and a glum expression.

"How are they treating you here, Felix?"

"Not bad, I guess, for jail."

"Lulu and Bert haven't been beating on you or anything like that, I take it."

"Nope."

"I suppose they'll leave that to the big boys. They like the newcomers to get a chance to feel comfortable for a while."

"What do you mean, 'the big boys'?"

"Oh, the rest of the inmates. They're always hungry for some new entertainment."

"Entertainment?"

"Oh, don't get me started on that, Felix. I haven't eaten supper yet. Now here's the deal I'm going to offer you. You give me truthful answers, something that helps me, and I'll talk to the judge and see if I can get you two guys sprung on your own recognizance."

"My what, Sheriff? I'm not sure I got one of those."

Tully stared at him. "Let's just say I'll try to get you released. I'm not promising anything. The judge and I don't exactly get along, but I'll try. Good enough?"

"Yeah, go ahead and ask."

Tully pondered his best approach, then said, "You recall your old friend Fletch, right, Felix?"

"Yeah, we had some good times together, Fletch and me. Then you sent him to the pen."

"Yes, I did, but you have to remember good times don't last forever, particularly when you are threatening to shoot people and rob them blind, entertaining as that might be."

"I never done none of that. Fletch liked to work alone."

"I know, Felix. That's why you're not in prison with him. Well, actually, Fletch isn't in prison himself at the moment. That's why I wanted to talk to you."

Felix stared at him, his eyes blinking. Tully smiled and cracked his knuckles. "My question to you is this. Have you heard from Fletch since he broke out of prison?" He could practically see the wheels turning in the man's head. "Stop trying to think up a lie, Felix, and tell me the truth."

"Yeah, I heard from him right after he busted out."

"And?"

"He's holed up in the house of a friend of his. The guy who lives there used to rob banks, but after his stretch in prison, I think he retired. He got released not too long ago."

Tully turned this over in his mind. "So maybe Fletch isn't far from the prison, if he's staying with his bank robber friend?"

"Yeah, but he's hot to get back to Blight. Says he has a debt to settle here. His problem, he ain't got a car. So he's going to hang out with his pal till he can figure out something."

Tully smiled. "Well, shoot, maybe I'll save him the trouble and drop down there for a visit. This bank-robbing friend of his have a name?"

"I'm sure he does, but I don't know it."

"Well, thanks for the info, Felix. I'll talk to the judge tomorrow and see if I can get you sprung."

"Wow! I'd appreciate it, Sheriff."

"Now I've got to go find myself some supper." He yelled for Bert to take care of Felix, then got up and left.

Chapter 18

The next morning Tully slept in and arrived at the courthouse an hour late, still munching the last of his Egg McMuffin. Daisy appeared to have already reached her frenetic phase. "So," he said, "did you get me the information I asked you to track down?"

Daisy heaved a sigh, perhaps of exasperation, and looked at a sheet of notes she had taken. "Yes, I did, and it wasn't easy. The board for state prisons recently paroled a bank robber now living at 805 North Pine Street in Wister, Idaho, if you've ever heard of it. Does that work for you, Boss?"

"It does indeed, Daisy. Now I have to get a flight to Wister."

"You think an airline flies into a burg as small as Wister?"

"The airline I'm thinking of does. It also allows passengers to carry loaded pistols and pump shotguns."

"Good heavens! Tell me the name, so I never fly on it!"

"Pete Reynolds."

"Oh, I should have known."

Tully smiled. "Yeah, but for this round-trip flight I think the county should at least pay Pete for the gas."

"How about something for Pete's time and trouble?"

"Oh, all right, Daisy, if you insist on throwing the county's money around like a drunken judge."

"It was only a suggestion, Boss."

Tully walked into his office, flopped down in his chair, and dialed the number for Pete Reynolds. Mrs. Reynolds answered. "Pete? Yes, he's still here, Bo. I suppose you want to talk to him."

"Yes, I do, Alice. I have a little chore for him."

"How did I guess? Hold on a sec."

Pete came on. "What now, Bo?"

"I need you to fly me down to the little town of Wister. There will be just you and me going down and, with any luck, three of us coming back."

"And when do you want to do this?"

"Tomorrow at noon, okay?"

"Good to see you're starting to plan ahead. And how much is the county willing to pay?"

"Two thousand for the round trip."

"Dollars?"

"Yes, dollars, Pete."

"All right then! Be out at the strip at noon. The county can buy you and me lunch at the Airport Café."

"It's a deal."

After hanging up, he asked Daisy to find him the phone number for Viola Hilligoss up in Pine Flats.

Sorting through her collection of phone books, she soon came up with the number. Tully dialed it.

"Oh, Sheriff Tully! How nice to hear from you!"

Tully leaned back in his chair and put his feet up on his desk. "The reason I'm calling, Viola, I just wanted to thank you for coming forward and clearing those two men of the crime of robbery."

"Oh, I was happy to do so, Sheriff. I've never been able to stand Clyde Parker anyway. But you know, the strangest thing happened. This nice young man who said he was a reporter for the *Silver Tip Miner* stopped by and interviewed me about the whole incident."

Tully's head sagged. "Was the nice young man fat?"

"Oh, I wouldn't say fat. Maybe a little pudgy. But he was so nice. He had me get in his car with him. We drove down to the General Store and he took a picture of me standing in front of it. He treated me just like I was a hero of some kind."

Tully's feet had hit the floor and he was now leaning forward with his arms pressed tensely against his desk. "Did the fat little man give you any indication of when he intended to print his story?"

"Oh, in this week's paper, I think. But that's not all, Sheriff. I told him what you did for the three young men, getting them those jobs down at the sawmill, and he said he would stop by there and interview Hank Schmitt, the foreman, and maybe take pictures of the three young men at work on the green chain."

Tully shuddered. "Well, thanks for the update, Viola." He hung up, spun around in his chair, and stared out the window. Two ice fishermen were sitting on wooden crates next to a hole in the ice. A year from now he would be out there with them. If August Finn showed up to interview him about how many fish he had caught, he would push him through the hole in the ice.

At noon the next day, Tully parked his Explorer in the Blight City airport parking lot and walked over to the café. Pete was already seated at a table, a cup of coffee in front of him. He looked up from the menu as Tully approached. "You know something, Bo, this little café here is one of the best-kept culinary secrets in all of Blight. The food is terrific."

Tully gave him a wary look as he pulled out a chair and sat down. "That would be a major secret, all right. Anything you recommend?"

"It's all good, but the California Scramble is my favorite—scrambled eggs, pieces of bacon, tomatoes, avocado, celery, and I don't know what all. Take the cinnamon toast with it for your bread."

"Sounds perfect, Pete."

The flight to the Wister airport took exactly two hours. Fortunately, the operator of the tiny airport had two vehicles he rented out, one of them an older panel truck with single seats for driver and passenger. The back of the truck was empty, except for a rear seat scavenged from an old car of some kind. "The truck looks a little beat up all right," the operator said, "but the engine is good."

"It better be," Tully said. "I may need it for a getaway."

"I hope you ain't planning on robbing something," the owner said.

"Naw," Tully said. "Not unless we have to stay here overnight."

The man gave them directions to North Pine Street. Twenty minutes later they were parked next to a mailbox on a post, the number 805 hand lettered on it in white paint.

"I hope you don't need any help with this part," Pete said.

Tully gave him his cold stare. "You brought a gun, didn't you?"

"I always bring a gun when I'm out with you, Bo. I just don't like having to use it."

"Is it loaded?"

"Yeah."

"Well, the guy who lives here, his name is Colin O'Mera. He's a bank robber who was released from prison not long ago. Now he could be charged with harboring an escaped prisoner and go back up for it. Do you get my drift, Pete?"

"Yeah. I guess I should ask for more details before I go flying off with you on these little adventures."

Tully stared across the front yard of the tiny house. "I'm going to walk over there and pound on the door in a minute. You sit here and watch. If you see the guy shoot me, you drive off and get help. Don't try to take him on yourself."

Pete stared at him. "You got to be kidding, Bo."

"I am. What I meant to say was, if shooting starts, don't drive off without me."

"I'm way ahead of you on that, Bo. I'll be a block away before the first shot is fired."

Tully shook his head, got out of the car, walked across the front yard, and knocked on the door. A tall, thin, fit-looking man answered. His hair was trimmed very short, as if still growing back in from a prison cut. He glared at Tully. "Yeah?"

"Sir," Tully said, "I was wondering if I might interest you in the purchase of a Handy Dandy vacuum cleaner."

The man's glare softened. "Matter of fact, I could use a vacuum."

Tully relaxed his grip on the leather bag of buckshot in his hip pocket.

"Actually, sir, I'm not a vacuum cleaner salesman. I'm sheriff of Blight County. I understand you have an escaped convict living with you. As a person just released from prison yourself, I'm sure you realize, Mr. O'Mera, you could be convicted again, this time of harboring an escaped felon. Now suppose you just turn him over to me and we forget any involvement you may have."

O'Mera thought about this. Then he smiled. In a low voice, he said, "I like your suggestion, Sheriff, and would be very happy to be relieved of my freeloading visitor, not that I have any knowledge he's an escaped convict."

"Of course not," Tully said.

"Wait here."

A minute later he dragged Fletch to the door, crammed an oversize hat on his head, and shoved him into Tully's arms. After snapping cuffs on Fletch, Tully nodded at the man. "Thank you very much, sir. I appreciate your cooperation."

"You sure I won't hear any more about this?" O'Mera said.

"You definitely won't. It's the Blight Way."

"The Blight Way? What's that?"

"It's a little too complicated for me to explain right now, but I assure you, sir, there's nothing more for you to worry about—provided, of course, you give up robbing banks."

O'Mera smiled at him. "There's always a catch, ain't there, Sheriff?"

"I'm afraid so."

They landed at the Blight City airport, Tully and Pete sitting in the cockpit seats, Fletch crouched on the old car seat behind them, a chain around his handcuffs and attached to an eyebolt in the floor.

Tully said, "It was thoughtful of you, Pete, to install that eyebolt. Saves me from holding a gun on our prisoner all the way back."

"The last time we made a flight, I figured I wasn't done with you yet, Bo, so I made a few adjustments in the plane."

"Next time, how about a little heater for brewing hot coffee?"

"Oh, by all means. I'll get right on that. So, how about my two grand?"

"No problem, Pete. The check will be in the mail first thing tomorrow. Or maybe the next day. Who knows about these things."

Back at the courthouse, Tully turned Fletch over to the night shift at the jail and went up to his office. The place was empty except for Augie Finn of the *Silver Tip Miner*, who sat in a chair next to Daisy's vacant desk.

"Cripes, Bo," Finn said, rubbing his eyes. "I thought you would never get back."

"Augie, if I knew you were here, I would never have come back. What do you want?"

"I just want to know why you flew off to Wister with Pete Reynolds."

Tully pulled out Daisy's chair and sank into it. "How on earth did you find out about my trip with Pete?"

Augie thought for a moment, as if wondering whether he should divulge a secret or not. Then he said, "Any time the sheriff of Blight County splurges on California Scramble for himself and the only decent pilot in Blight City, it gets my attention. Something has to be going on. So what is it, Bo?"

Tully's shoulders sagged in surrender. He couldn't even eat anything without Augie finding out what it was. He told him about the capture and return of Fletch to the Blight County jail. He filled the editor in on the criminal's record, while Augie scribbled furiously.

"Bo, this is the best story I've had since Fester's murder."

Tully laughed. "You know I do everything I can, Augie, to keep the *Silver Tip Miner* in business. So I would think you might try to be less of a thorn in my side. By the way, how did you learn about the California Scramble?"

Augie laughed. "I can't reveal my sources, Bo, you know that."

"Has to be one of the waitresses at the Airport Café."

"Airport Café? Can't say I've ever dined there and spread around major tips to the girls. Anyway, Bo, thanks for the story."

Chapter 19

Tully arrived at the office at seven the next morning and was surprised to see his father sitting in the same office the old man had once run with an iron if somewhat corrupt fist.

Tully walked in. "Pap! What are you doing here? Looks as if you've taken over the show and are running it."

Pap smiled. He was still handsome when cleaned up a bit. His gray hair curled up around his ears in a way that seemed to appeal to the ladies, even if he was nearly eighty years old. "I come to solve your murder mystery for you, Bo."

Tully grabbed one of the visitor chairs, spun it around, folded his arms on the rounded back, and stared at his father from in front of his own desk.

"That must have been quite a feat, since you know practically nothing about it."

"I know plenty about it. I plied Lurch with drink last night and he brought me up to date on all the grisly details. Nothing I like better than a grisly detail. Plus, I had helped Lurch find most of his clues out at the Fester murder site. Then when I got home, I couldn't stop thinking about them."

Tully sighed, leaned back in his chair, and stared up at his office's ceiling tiles.

Pap's eyes narrowed into mean little slits. "You better be listening to this, Bo, because I ain't repeating it."

"Promise?"

"No. Now shut up and listen. Lurch checked every airline in the vicinity but never found one that claimed to have a Mrs. Fester on it in the last six months."

"I know that, Pap."

"Yeah, but somehow the lady Fester got herself to Mexico, because you talked to her there in Cabo San Lucas."

"This office leaks like a sieve," Bo growled. "I'll have to have a talk with my CSI unit."

"You leave that boy alone, Tully. He's the best thing you got going for you."

"So, what's your theory, Pap? I have lots of actual sheriff stuff to do today."

"Okay, but pay attention now, because I don't want to run through this twice. According to everything we've found out, Mrs. Fester left for Mexico the same day Fester got hisseff killed. The snow Lurch and me turned up was the same snow that fell on Fester when he got shot with that arrow. Now follow me on this, Bo."

Tully sighed. "I'm following."

"Okay then. Someone from the ranch up here gets in a three-quarter-ton, four-wheel-drive pickup truck that belongs to Hillory Fester or is at least used by her as if it's her car. It belongs to the ranch, so I guess in a way it is her car. Anyway, early in the morning long before Fester gets up to go eagle shooting, somebody drives Hillory out to the knoll and drives into the skid trail on the far side of the woods, stopping where the truck tracks ended, the ones Lurch and me found under the last snow. Hillory gets out with her bow and arrow and tramps through the snow to the middle of the woods, where she builds a fire to keep warm. The driver of the pickup backs out and returns to the ranch, maybe even climbs into bed for a quick snooze. All this is done at around four o'clock in the morning while the snow is falling. At about six a.m., Fester gets up, drives to the knoll, and turns around at the skid trail. Those are the tracks that show someone turned in a short ways and backed out. After he's turned around, he drives back next to the knoll and parks his vehicle at the edge of the road. Then he gets out to shoot eagles. Hillory, let's say, hears the truck stop. She kicks some snow over her fire and starts walking through the woods toward the knoll. After she sees Fester pass by, she waits a bit and then steps out and shoots him in the back with the arrow. As the tracks show, she then walks back through the woods to the skid trail where she meets the driver of her pickup, who has come back and stopped where the tracks end. They back out of the skid trail and drive to Morg's truck. The accomplice gets out, climbs into Morg's truck, and drives it back to the ranch. It's snowing hard by that time and they expect the body will soon be covered up and won't be discovered till spring. Hillory backs up into the skid trail, turns right, and drives her truck to Mexico. That's why there ain't no record of her flying on a plane and why there ain't no truck at the Fester ranch matching the tire tread of the truck at the killing. So what do you think of that theory, Bo?"

Tully blinked at Pap. Then he grabbed the back of his chair and pushed himself as far back from the old man as he could get. "That's just about the way I've got it figured, Pap."

"I bet."

The phone rang. Pap picked it up, listened, and then said, "Please hold all phone calls, Daisy. Bo will get back to them shortly."

Tully rolled his eyes. Pap got up and walked to the door, where he turned to Tully, who sat staring across his own desk at his empty chair. "Oh, one more thing, Bo. I don't want Lurch getting into any trouble asking for my assistance. You understand?"

Tully stood up and moved around the desk. "Gotcha, Pap. Many thanks for your help on this. I never could have figured it all out by myself."

"No problem, Bo." Pap strode out through the office and down the hallway, the *klocking* of his cowboy boots fading into the distance.

Tully settled into his office chair, the warmth of the seat making him shudder. He picked up the phone. "Daisy! Get your butt in here!"

Daisy burst in, notepad in her hand. "I'm sorry, Boss. Your dad is just one of those people I can't say no to."

Tully stared at her. "I realize that. Where's Lurch? I want to have a word with him."

"He fled as soon as he saw your dad headed for your office. He may be on a bus on his way out of state by now."

Tully shook his head as if in exasperation. "Get him on his cell phone and tell him to get back to the office. He's not in any trouble. I'm well aware of how imposing my old man can be when he wants to know something. As a matter of fact, I think he and Lurch have a pretty good idea of what went down at the knoll. Besides, I should have known better than to leave Lurch alone with someone like Pap."

Tully arrived at the office at seven the next morning and was surprised to see the Unit already hunched over his computer. "Hey, Lurch, get over here. I've got a theory to run by you."

Lurch followed him into his office, grabbed one of the chairs in front of Tully's desk, spun it around, straddled it, and rested his arms on the back. "What's up, Boss?"

"I've got a theory about Fester's murder."

"I love your theories. Run it by me, Boss."

"First, you never found an airline that would admit to flying Hillory Fester as a passenger."

"None."

"Okay, consider this. Say Hillory Fester left for Mexico the same day Morg disappeared and, according to your estimate, the same day he was killed."

"Yeah, based on Pap's and my estimate of the time of the first snowfall on the knoll and what the foreman at the ranch told you."

Lurch sat for a long minute, apparently thinking the theory over. Then he said, "Does this mean I get to fly to Mexico, Boss?"

"It means exactly that, Lurch."

"Good. I can use a vacation. Besides, I've never been to Mexico. You got any idea who the accomplice was?"

"Jeff Sheridan."

"That would be my guess," Lurch said. "Maybe Sheridan was the shooter. Maybe Mrs. Fester wasn't there at all. But I think the tracks indicate they were made by either Jeff Sheridan or Mrs. Fester, someone with fairly small feet."

Lurch appeared lost in thought for several seconds. Tully wondered what aspect of the crime concerned him. Then Lurch said, "I can't wait to try an authentic Mexican taco, Boss."

Tully sighed. "I'll make sure you have a good time in Mexico, Lurch. You deserve it. But a gringo like you should never eat anything in Mexico that comes wrapped in a tortilla, at least not something from a street vendor. My first trip there I ate a taco from a street vendor as soon as I got off the plane. It was so delicious I scarcely minded the month I spent in a hospital afterward. So don't eat anything from street vendors."

Lurch jumped up from his chair. "I'd better go home and pack."

"There's no rush. I've got another irritation I have to take care of first."

Chapter 20

Tully stopped by the district attorney's office. "Hi, Opel," he said to the head secretary, who had her own two secretaries. Someday he had to figure out how to get a setup like this. "Leroy available?"

"Gosh, Bo, he's out of the office. He should be back soon. Grab a chair, and I'll get you a cup of coffee. Cream or sugar?"

"How about both?"

"You got it." Opel walked into a little room off the DA's office and soon returned with a tray containing a cup of coffee, a doughnut, cream, and sugar. Yes, he would definitely have to work on a setup like this. He watched her set the tray on the edge of her desk, walk around to her chair, and sit down. She was quite attractive. Tully pulled his chair over to the desk and sat across from her. "Opel, you want to do another favor for me, while I'm waiting for Leroy?"

"Anything, Bo."

"Call the prison in Boise and tell them that if they're looking for an escaped convict by the name of George Mahoney, I have him locked up in Blight County Jail."

"No kidding?"

"Yep, no kidding. I locked George up here yesterday."

She made the call and told whoever answered, "Yes, George Mahoney. Sheriff Bo Tully is sitting right here, if you wish to speak to him." She looked at Tully. "He wants to speak to you."

Tully took the phone. "This is Sheriff Tully."

"Bo, this is Frank Pile. I'm a captain of guards here at the prison. The lady says you have George Mahoney locked up for us."

"Yes, I do, Frank. He's kind of a threat to me personally, running around loose. If he gets out again, I'll probably just shoot him and put an end to the nuisance."

"You won't hear any complaints from me if you do. I'll have a couple of guards come up and relieve you of him. After this breakout, I don't think he'll see the light of day for a very long time."

"Good to hear it, Frank. He's got kind of a grudge against me, I don't know why, and I have enough trouble watching my back as it is."

"I know the feeling well. Thanks for your help, Bo."

"No trouble."

He hung up. "Thanks, Opel. I guess we've got that little problem taken care of."

Just then the district attorney walked in. "Bo! Good of you to stop by. Step into my office. I've got some stuff to discuss with you." He held the door for Tully and closed it behind him. Sitting down at his desk, he leaned back in his chair and heaved a sigh. Tully pulled up a chair and sat down in front of the desk. "Guess what," Fagan said. "The FBI has sent some agents in to check on rumors that our judges have been taking payoffs from lawyers."

Tully shook his head. "What on earth is wrong with the feds? They know this is Blight County. Have they no respect for our traditions?"

Fagan frowned at him. "This is serious, Bo."

"I suppose it is, Leroy. You would think the FBI would have better things to do than get involved in such trivial matters. I certainly have no personal knowledge of our judges throwing cases because of payoffs. Do you?"

Fagan frowned but didn't answer. "This could be serious, Bo. People could go to prison."

"I suppose. It so happens I know one of the FBI agents sent here to check on the rumors. I'll ask her what she thinks of such suspicions and what nut is raising them. As a matter of fact, I will stop by and talk to old Judge Patterson, to see if he has any suspects among his fellow judges."

"Patterson! He would be my most likely suspect!"

"Mine, too. There's no point in questioning people you know are innocent. They never have a clue. Patterson may at least point me in the right direction, should the FBI lean on me to get involved. You sure you're clean, Leroy?"

"The cleanest DA Blight County ever had."

"That leaves a lot of room."

"I suppose, but I'm happy with my salary," Fagan said. "My wife and kids would flip if I ever got involved in any dirty stuff, tempting as it might be."

"Wife and kids can be such a pain. As you know, Leroy, I don't have any. I do miss my wife, though."

"You'll never find another woman like Ginger, Bo."

"I suppose they're out there, but I've never come across one. By the way, Leroy, do you know what gives the FBI an angle on our judges?"

Fagan frowned. "I'm not sure. The agent in charge says they've turned up a secret bank account belonging to a lawyer, and the cash in the account has never had taxes paid on it. Don't ask me how they figure out something like that. On the other hand, what do lawyers need secret accounts for, except to pay off judges?"

"Take the family to Disney World?" Tully said. "A vacation in Hawaii? Simple things like that?"

"Yeah, right. The lead agent tells me she's worked with you before."

"A couple of murders. Nothing serious, but you know the FBI."

"She's very attractive."

"Oh yeah, there's that. I probably should go track her down, before she gets some of our citizens in trouble. She's quite tenacious."

Chapter 21

Tully pulled up in front of Judge Patterson's house and got out. Patterson's Cadillac was in the driveway. Tully shook his head. Judges should not drive Cadillacs, particularly in Blight County. They are a dead giveaway. He walked up on the porch and rang the doorbell. Mrs. Patterson answered.

"Why, Bo! So good to see you. You need to drop by more often."

"Been busy, Mildred. Up to my neck in crime. Is His Holiness in?"

"Yes, I'm sorry to say. Otherwise, you and I could have a high old time. He just replenished his secret stash. I'll whip us each up a martini."

"Better make one for the judge, too. Otherwise, he'll get suspicious."

"You think so, Bo? Aren't you ashamed, trying to flatter an old lady like me? I do love it, though. And you, too, of course."

"I'm getting old, Mil, but my eyesight is good. You're still as beautiful as ever. Don't know how you do it."

"Magic, Bo, magic. You go in the study, dear, and rest yourself in your favorite chair, and I'll run down the judge."

Tully had scarcely eased himself into his favorite rocker in the judge's study when the old man came bustling in.

"Bo! Bo! What's this I hear about the FBI's being in town?"

"Nothing for you to concern yourself about, Judge. The agents have just turned up some nonsense about a secret bank account."

"Oh, good heavens!" The judge slumped into a chair and put his hands to the sides of his face. "How on earth did they find out about something like that?"

"To tell you the truth, I don't have a clue, but I suspect they leaned on one of the bank managers or picked up a rumor of some kind that apparently led them to the bank account. You know bank people can't be trusted to keep their mouths shut. They're always blabbing about something, and apparently the agents picked up a lead of some kind. Nothing for you to worry about, Judge."

"Easy for you to say, Bo."

Tully smiled. "The FBI thoroughly disapproves of the Blight Way when it comes to law enforcement. They always want me to stick to all the piddling rules. Which reminds me, I've got a couple of our citizens in jail on a minor-endangerment charge. That situation has now passed, because a few days in jail should have taught them a lesson. They also helped relieve me of a dangerous threat to my well-being, in exchange for an offer I made them."

"And that offer is?"

"I told them I'd talk to you about dismissing the charges. Sure, there were about thirty witnesses to the knife fight, but maybe we could view the knife fight as just playing around. What do you say, Judge?"

Mildred scurried in with three martinis on a tray and passed one each to Tully and the judge. She then took hers and seated herself in an easy chair in the corner.

The judge said, "Is this, by any chance, the incident I heard about where you knocked both fighters cold with a single swipe of your blackjack?"

Tully took a sip of his martini. Perfect. One thing about Mil, she knew how to make a drink. A few sips by the judge and the old man should give him anything he asked for.

The judge sipped his drink. "So what's the minor-endangerment situation, Bo?"

"That knife fight down at Slade's Bar & Grill."

The judge stared at him. "Oh yes, the knife fight. In this day and age? I can't believe it. They must be stupid."

"Of course they're stupid, Judge. If stupidity was a crime, half the people in Blight County would be locked up. But one of these guys told me the whereabouts of an escaped convict who had threatened to kill me."

"Good heavens, Bo! How did you find out about the threat?"

"From my fortune-teller."

"Oh, Etta Gorsich! She's one of the best. I use her sometimes when I have a tough decision to make."

"You can't go wrong with Etta, Judge."

After the judge had finished his martini, Tully handed him the release forms he had made out and the judge scrawled his signature on them without bothering to read either the fine or large print.

"Thanks, Judge. I owe you one."

"You owe me about a hundred, but keep me informed about what those FBI agents are up to. I've never trusted the feds."

"Me neither, Judge. Anything turns up, I'll let you know. Of course, Leroy Fagan is involved, too."

"The DA? Is he a suspect?"

"Just an intensely interested observer, I think, but who knows?"

Later that day, Tully stopped by the jail. "Lulu, please haul Milton and Felix out here for me."

"You gonna work 'em over, Bo?"

"Naw. We made a deal and they kept their part of the bargain, so I'm keeping mine. I've got an order from the judge here dismissing the charges against them."

Lulu laughed. "Bo, if you ain't got that old man wrapped around your little finger, I don't know what."

Tully smiled. "I know that, Lulu, and you know that, but let's just keep it a secret between you and me."

Lulu drew a finger across her lips to indicate they were sealed. She yelled at Bert and the big assistant

jailer came rushing over. "Haul them two knife fighters out here, Bert. Bo got them released."

Bert shook his head. "I don't understand, Bo. You're
the one arrested them."

"Yeah, but they did me a big favor, maybe saved my
life. So I'm just paying them back the favor."

Bert walked back into the block and said some-
thing to two of the occupants. Seconds later Felix and
Milton came scurrying out. "Sheriff!" Felix blurted.
"You kept your word!"

"Yep, I always keep my word. You perhaps noticed
a new resident in the cell block."

"Yeah! Ole Fletch. I hope he don't know . . ."

"You won't have to worry about Ole Fletch for a
very long time. Some prison guards will be picking
him up soon and hauling him back to the joint. By the
time he gets out again, we'll all be too old to care. So
pack up your stuff and clear out of here."

Tully watched them scurry back to their cells to pick
up their belongings. He sighed and shook his head.
Then he glanced at Lulu. She was watching him, smiling and shaking her head.

Chapter 22

Daisy was busy on her phone when Tully walked in. "Hank Schmitt on line one for you, Boss."

Tully walked into his office and picked up the phone. "Hank, good to hear from you. How are our criminals doing?"

"They're hard as nails, Bo. Spent the day pulling ten-inch planks off the green chain and never took a break. I took them out to breakfast the other morning and asked them about their plans. All three are headed back to college. May even try out for the football team. Or at least wrestling. Be a shame to waste all that new muscle."

Tully nodded. "Nothing like the green chain to fill a young fellow full of enthusiasm for college. I wish someone had put me on it when I was their age. Too late for that now."

"It's never too late for college, Bo. Hardly a day goes by I don't think about going back."

"You'd probably major in forestry, Hank, something practical like that, where you could ride around the woods in a green pickup truck all day. I regret not majoring in forestry myself, instead of art."

"Well, I heard from Daisy a while back you just sold a painting for twelve thousand dollars! That sounds pretty dang practical to me."

"Yeah, you're right about that. I don't know how practical painting pictures is, but I'm going to retire from sheriffing pretty soon and give it a shot full-time, eight hours a day. Maybe after that I'll want to hit you up for a job on the green chain."

Hank laughed. "I doubt that. First you may want to ask these three boys about it. Here's an odd thing about that. This pudgy little fellow by the name of August Finn showed up, interviewed me about how you arranged the job for the boys and like that, took pictures of me and the three boys, each of them standing down by the green chain. You know this Finn fellow, Bo?"

"Yeah. Anyway, Hank, thanks for taking care of our three criminals. I appreciate it." He hung up.

He glanced across the briefing room. Lurch was hunched over his computer, typing madly away. Probably an email to some girl. He punched a button on his phone. Lurch answered. "Yeah, Boss."

"Get your butt in here. I have something to discuss with you."

He watched as his CSI unit calmly shut down his computer and sauntered across the briefing room.

Somehow he had never been able to instill fear in any of his staff.

Lurch opened the door, walked in, and grabbed a chair across from him, spun it around, sat down, and propped his elbows on its rounded back. It seemed as if none of his staff, except maybe Daisy, could merely sit in a chair. "Yeah, Boss?"

Tully stood up, turned, and stared out over the lake for a minute. He could see the two fishermen hunched over a hole in the ice. Lucky devils. He hoped they both froze. He turned back to Lurch. "Pap gave me a rundown on how you and he figured the murder of Morg Fester. I don't like it, but I think you may be right."

"What don't you like, Boss?"

"I don't like Hillory Fester being the killer. Or Jeff Sheridan, either, for that matter."

Lurch nodded. "We didn't like it, either. But the boot tracks of the killer indicated a small foot, a woman's foot. What other woman was involved with Fester?"

"Dozens of them. Some had boyfriends, some had husbands. Any one of those women might have done him just to shut him up about their affair."

Tully sat back down in his office chair and turned it around to face the Unit. "But you and Pap may be right, Lurch. A woman could have killed him, all right. She would have to be fairly sturdy, to pull a forty-pound bow and hold the arrow squarely on the target. Some cooks and waitresses have arms like that." He didn't mention one particular chef who came to mind.

"Yeah," Lurch said. "And the arrow was of a length commonly used by a woman."

"I know. We have no proof, of course, that Hillory was involved. The fact she left for Mexico the same day Fester disappeared is an odd coincidence. I did check her closet for a pair of hiking boots and didn't find any. Jeff Sheridan told me she had a pair that she wore on her hikes in the woods, and he thought she must have taken them to Mexico with her. Apparently, she likes to explore the desert next to the ranch and probably wears them then. She might even have worn boots to drive that pickup to Mexico. We seem to have some convergences here, Lurch."

"Convergences?"

"Never mind. Maybe I meant coincidences. You can't base a murder on coincidences, though. How do you feel about taking that trip to Mexico we talked about before?"

"I'd love it! Anything in particular I'd look for?"

"A three-quarter-ton four-wheel-drive pickup with a tread that matches the tracks on the skid trail."

"And I'd find it where in Mexico?"

"Either in the parking lot of a fancy hotel in Cabo San Lucas or on a huge ranch east of Cabo a couple hundred miles. Let's hope you find it at the Cabo hotel. Otherwise, you'll have to take the ferry across to the mainland."

Lurch stood up, a big grin on his face. "When do I leave, Boss?"

"Go home and start packing. First, have Daisy check with the airlines to find out what's required for you to carry a firearm on a plane as a law enforcement officer. Also, find out from the border patrol what you need to carry a firearm into Mexico."

"I'll get right on it. Is Pap going, too? I like working with him. He figured out a whole bunch of the stuff at the crime scene."

Tully rubbed his throbbing temples as he stared at the Unit. "I guess so. I would never live it down if Pap didn't work the final phase of the hunt. Have Daisy order the tickets. Right now I've got to drive out to the Fester ranch and get somebody to draw me a map to the Mexico ranch. You might need it if Hillory isn't at the hotel in Cabo. I notice she didn't make it back to Blight for Morg's funeral."

"I didn't make it, either," Lurch said. "How about you, Boss?"

"Yeah, I did. Probably the smallest funeral in the whole history of funerals. I doubt Morg was a bit upset, though. Probably smiled with satisfaction. I didn't notice because it was a closed casket."

"You're giving me the creeps, Boss." The Unit left. Tully sat pondering the venture. It would be bad if it failed and worse if it succeeded.

He got up and wandered out to the briefing room, looking for Daisy. He found her fingering her way through files in a cabinet. "I just gave Lurch a job that may be too much for him. He and Pap are flying to Cabo San Lucas, Mexico. Help him out with the tickets, hotel reservation, rental car, weapons permits, all that stuff."

"Sure, Boss. I'm already checking on the tickets. The rest shouldn't take much longer than all night and half of tomorrow."

"Good."

Chapter 23

Tully pulled into the Fester ranch and parked by the bunkhouse. He walked over and knocked on the door. Wiggens answered. "Sheriff Tully! Come on in, sir!"

"Thank you, Mr. Wiggens. Is Jeff Sheridan around?"

"No, sir. He's off at the Mexico ranch."

"Great," Tully said. "Well, maybe you can help me. You ever been down to that ranch, Wiggens?"

"Yes, sir, a couple of times."

"Do you think you could draw me a map of how to get there from here, along with any directions you can think of? By the way, Wiggens, do you have a first name?"

"Yeah. Harold."

"Harold Wiggens," Tully said. "So, anyway, about the map, Wiggens, can you draw one that will show me how to get to the ranch?"

"Sure." He sat down at the bunkhouse table and began to sketch the map. Tully sat next to him and watched him draw. Wiggens said, "I reckon you would want to fly from Blight City down to Tucson. Otherwise, it's a pretty long haul. Rent a car in Tucson and drive south on Highway 19. Cross the border at Nogales." He printed out the name "Nogales" next to a large dot he drew on the US-Mexico border. Another line showed Highway 19 headed south. "About forty miles south of the border you'll come to the ranch. It's on both sides of the highway." He drew two boxes on each side of Highway 19 and printed "Fester Ranch" on each of them. On the left one he sketched some tiny rectangles that Tully supposed represented buildings. "This here is the headquarters. Big signs identify the ranch, so you shouldn't miss it. You come to Hermosillo, you've passed it."

"Perfect, Wiggens!" he said. "So Mr. Sheridan is down there right now?"

"Yeah. I think maybe Jeff and Hillory are going to get married down there, maybe right on the ranch. She's already driven over from Cabo."

"Married! Really? Well, I did notice Hillory didn't make it back for Morg's funeral."

"Yeah. You didn't see me there, either. The way he treated Hillory, I'm not surprised she wasn't there. He didn't treat me much better, but Jeff got along with him okay. I guess he probably needed Jeff more than he needed me."

Tully started to leave and then stopped and turned. "By the way, Wiggens, do you happen to know if there's an extra key around here for the pickup Mrs. Fester drives?"

Wiggens straightened up, his brow furrowed. "An extra key for her pickup, Sheriff?"

"Yeah, I know that sounds strange, but it's sort of a cop thing. Can you help me out?"

"Well, yeah, I think so. Wait here and I'll check." He returned a few minutes later with a key. "We keep all the extra pickup keys on a board out back."

"Thanks a lot, Wiggens. Let's keep this just between you and me. Maybe I can do you a favor sometime."

Wiggens smiled. "I'll probably need one."

Chapter 24

When Tully got back to the office, Brian Pugh was waiting for him. Right away he knew trouble was afoot, because Pugh never bothered him unless it was. Daisy was on the phone with someone, absent-mindedly scratching her head with a pencil. He gave her a squeeze on the shoulder as he walked past. He glanced back to make sure he had gotten a smile. He had. Pugh at least wasn't sitting at Tully's desk or straddling a chair but sitting in one in a normal fashion. Normal was getting to be something Tully appreciated.

"What's up, Brian?"

"We've got a problem, Boss."

"Don't we always?"

"Yeah, but this one's kind of sad. You know crazy old Ed Stokes? His cabin sits just inside the line between Blight and Kindle Counties."

"Sure. I know Ed well. He's crazy as a bedbug but a nice enough fellow. Most crazy folks I know are pretty decent. I think our world nowadays makes them crazy. So what's he up to?"

"Well, come this afternoon, he's likely to be thrown in jail. He's in jail right now, but he's got a hearing before Judge Green at two this afternoon."

"A hearing?"

"Yeah. A couple of days ago, Sunday, I think it was, four cars full of high school kids roared into that open dirt space Ed calls a yard in front of his cabin and started doing wheelies, going round and round and terrorizing Ed's free-range chickens something awful. Well, you know how much Ed loves those chickens. Never kills one for food but just lets them die of old age, then buries them out behind his henhouse with a little board at the head of the grave with the chicken's name on it. So Ed whips out that big old .44 Magnum pistol of his and kills all four cars right there in his front yard."

"Kills their cars?"

"Yeah. Shot a hole through the hood and into the engine block of each one. The dang things practically exploded. The kids all jumped out screaming bloody mercy and ran for the woods, leaving their cars dead and smoking there in Ed's yard. The next day Vernon Cave drove his wrecker out there. Ed was sitting on his porch in his rocking chair. Vernon gives him a little wave and Ed nods back. Then Vernon hooks up one of the cars and tows it away. Then he comes back and gets the other cars, one by one, and tows them back to town. Ed never gave him a bit of trouble, except for raising a few beads of sweat on Vernon's forehead. Well, of course, the kids blab to their fathers, all dentists and lawyers and store managers, uppity folk like that, city fathers and all, and they get Kindle County Sheriff Walt Messman, along with some state patrolmen, to go out and arrest Ed and haul him off to jail. So he's been sitting in a Kindle jail cell all day and a night with nobody to stand up for him."

Tully slumped into his chair, rested his elbows on his desk, and propped his chin on his folded hands. He stared at Pugh for a long moment of silence. Then he said, "What time's the hearing?"

"Two o'clock."

"I'll take care of it, Brian. I may need you to go along for backup."

"You think you'll need backup, Bo?"

"Only if Judge Green doesn't do what I tell him."

Chapter 25

Tully and Pugh walked into Judge Green's court-room shortly after two o'clock. Old Ed was standing up in front of the bench and the judge was glowering down at him. Tully unlocked the little gate in the front of the courtroom and walked through. Pugh followed him.

Judge Green straightened in his chair. "Sheriff Tully! What are you doing here?"

"I came to rescue one of my county residents, ille-gally arrested in my county. No one bothered to con-sult me."

The judge gave an uneasy glance at one of the state patrolmen. "I think the state has some jurisdiction there, Bo."

"Not without consulting me, they don't. These cow-boys are aware they're supposed to consult me first on any charge other than a traffic ticket. Judge, I've known

Ed Stokes all my life, and he's never once violated any law I know of. He lives alone out there in his little cabin in the woods and never takes a dime from the county, the state, or the US government. He grows all his own food, cuts his own firewood, and earns a bit of money gathering wild mushrooms, berries, and wild honey. Sells them to local restaurants. He knows a few bee trees nobody else has ever been able to find and is probably the only source of wild honey in the whole state. He doesn't kill anything. His chickens die only of old age and hawks, and he buries them out behind his chicken coop with little head markers. Their eggs furnish him with most of his protein. Then suddenly these spoiled teenage hoodlums roar onto his property and start doing wheelies in the dirt he calls his front yard. Their fancy cars roar about scaring the daylights out of Ed's chickens. If he had wanted to, instead of shooting their cars, Ed could have shot one or two of the laughing punks just for the heck of it, but he let them go. The next day Vernon Cave from Cave Wrecking makes several trips out to Ed's place to haul off the dead cars. Ed and Vernon had a cup of tea together. My point is, Ed is not a dangerous man."

The judge sighed. "Well, Bo, you do make some sense. But you have to admit shooting cars dead is evidence of insanity."

"Judge, if crazy was illegal, half the residents of these two counties would be in jail."

The judge nodded. "I can't argue that point with you, Sheriff, but . . ." Suddenly he stopped and stared into the courtroom. Tully turned and looked. There was Augie Finn, the editor and only reporter of the *Silver Tip Miner*, scribbling furiously away. The judge seemed to recover from his momentary trance. He said, "As an elected official, I'm not going to argue that point with you, Sheriff, but I'll tell you what I am going to do. Because it appears Ed Stokes was arrested illegally in your county, I'm turning him over to you. From now on, he's your problem."

"Good, Judge. I'll make sure he goes to jail for a while, just to teach him a lesson."

"Seems fair enough."

"C'mon, Ed," Tully said, taking the old man by the arm. "You're going to jail."

"Jail! What about my chickens, Bo?"

"Don't worry. I'll see they get fed. And I won't close the door on your jail cell, so you can get up and walk around any time you like. You can tell stories to the other prisoners and entertain them. We'll keep you just long enough to fatten you up and until tempers cool down over the cars you killed. How does that sound?"

"Sounds like the Blight Way," Pugh put in.

Augie Finn scooped up his papers and rushed out the door. Tully turned to Pugh and said, "I think we just made the front page of the *Silver Tip Miner* again."

Pugh stared after the pudgy little reporter. "That can't be all bad, can it, Bo?"

Tully shook his head. "Hard to tell about Augie."

Chapter 26

Once he had old Ed settled into his open cell, Tully introduced him to the other inmates, so he could wander around and talk to them. He ordered up a special meal from the kitchen for him. Ed was already out chatting with the various prisoners, who seemed pleased with the distraction. The kitchen staff had gone out of their way to prepare a special plate for him. The old man seemed pleased by it—so much so, in fact, that Tully thought he might never get rid of him. He then went back to his office, signaling for Lurch to follow him.

Lurch sauntered in, spun a chair around from the wall, and straddled it. "What's up, Boss?"

"You ready to go to Mexico?"

"Any time, Boss."

"Apparently, instead of returning here for her husband's funeral, Hillory drove her pickup from Cabo over to the Festers' Mexican ranch. Harold Wiggens drew me a map of how to get to the ranch. He said Hillory and Jeff Sheridan plan to get married there." He handed the map to Lurch.

The Unit frowned. "Married? Boss, this could almost be a . . ."

"Motive for murdering her husband," Tully said. "I'm way ahead of you on that, Lurch. What I'm trying to figure out is if it's okay to murder your husband if he's standing in your way of marrying someone you're actually in love with."

Lurch seemed to have trouble turning this over in his mind. Tully leaned back in his chair and gave the Unit a couple of seconds to sort through the complications. Then he said, "Now here's what I want you to do. Fly down to Tucson, then you and Pap rent a car and drive to the Mexican ranch. Hillory's pickup should be there. Take your mold and photos and see if you can get a match with the tread on one of her pickup tires. If you do, I want you to take that tire off her truck, put on its spare, and put the tire with the tread match in the bed of her pickup, so it doesn't get any more wear."

"Gotcha, Boss. Put the tire with the matching tread in the bed of her pickup. If her tread matches the mold and the one in the photo, we can place Mrs. Fester and probably Jeff at the scene and time of the murder. And now we've got a motive. What then?"

Tully stared at him. "I don't know. I'll notify the Mexican Federales what you're doing and they'll probably assign an officer to assist you. If not, they shouldn't bother you for stealing the pickup. Daisy will get you and Pap the airline tickets to Tucson and whatever documents you need to carry weapons over the border as US police officers."

Lurch appeared confused. "Pap?"

"Yes, Pap. He can come in handy, if things suddenly get rough. Daisy will take care of his tickets and documents, too."

Lurch shook his head as if to clear it. "If I get a match, do you want me to arrest Hillory or both her and Jeff and bring them back?"

"No, just see if you can get a match between the tread on the pickup and your mold without being detected. Then get out of there with her pickup and the tire. I'll arrange later for the Federales to take Hillory and Jeff into custody, once you're back in the States with the evidence. We can bring them back later."

"How are we going to steal Hillory's pickup? We don't have a key."

"Pap could probably handle that for you, but just in case . . ." He reached in his pocket, pulled out a key, and handed it to Lurch.

The deputy stared at it. "You are absolutely amazing, Boss!"

"I like to think so."

"Another thing, what if somebody catches me stealing Hillory's tire?"

Tully thought about this, then said, "Just do what you always do, Lurch."

"What's that?"

"Lie. Now here's the thing. If you get a match, let Pap return the rental car and you drive the pickup.

You can meet up in Nogales and spend the night at a motel, something on the poorer side of town. This isn't a vacation jaunt you're on, much as you would like to try out one of those fancy Mexican hotels. You can return the rental car in Tucson and you and Pap ride back in the truck."

"Uh, what if I get arrested for stealing the truck?"

I understand Mexican jails are quite cozy places, and we'll send you care packages until you're released, whenever that might be."

"I don't like the sound of this."

Tully laughed. "I'm only kidding you, Lurch. I'll call the local police so they understand what's going on. I'll make arrangements with all the proper authorities."

Lurch got up to leave. "I hope you'll have all this thought through, Boss, before Pap and I fly off to Tucson."

"It'll be a piece of cake, Lurch. Nothing for you and Pap to miss a minute of sleep over."

Chapter 27

The Unit left. Tully spun his chair around and gazed out over the frozen lake at the ice fishermen. This time next year he would be out there himself. He would paint in the evenings, of course, if none of his favorite TV programs were on. During the day, he would put on snowshoes and tramp around in his woods, possibly looking for a buckskin tamarack he could fell for firewood. He would saw the tree into firewood lengths with his razor-sharp crosscut saw, because the chain saw would make far too much noise. That reminded him that he would have to buy a cant hook or a log jack, something to handle the tree once he got it lying down on the ground. He hadn't seen a cant hook or a log jack in years and hoped somebody still sold them. Then . . . someone rapped on his door window. He glanced up: Angie Phelps was standing there, smiling in at him, her shoulder bag hanging from a strap down next to her right hand. He knew a loaded pistol was in the bag. She opened the door and stepped in.

"Angie!" he cried.

"Bo! It's so good to see you!"

Tully leaped out of his chair and gave the FBI agent a hug that lifted her nearly off her feet. Daisy frowned up at him from her desk. He shut the door. Angie seated herself primly in one of the chairs. "Bo, I shouldn't tell you this, but whatever you've been doing, stop it! You look plumb worn out."

Tully walked around his desk and sat down in his chair. "I heard you were back in town, Angie, to arrest some of our judges. I must say it's about time. They've raised their fees so high an average citizen like me can hardly afford one."

Angie smiled and shook her head. "Odd you should mention that. Some of our accountants have detected large amounts of cash stashed in local banks. It appears no federal taxes have been paid on that cash. So here we are, just to check everything out and see what's legitimate and what isn't. So, what have you been up to, Bo?"

"Oh, just the usual. Sheriffing mostly, but I just sold a watercolor for a substantial sum, and it looks as if I can now retire and make a living from my painting."

"That's wonderful, Bo!"

"So what have you been up to, other than fighting crime around the country?"

"Well, I got a promotion," Angie said. "I'm now stationed permanently in Idaho and am agent in charge of the top half of the state."

"Wow. Now I can retire happy, knowing that Blight County will be in your capable hands."

"Blight County," the agent said. "The very name makes me shudder. I know you like to do things a little differently here, Bo, but from now on there will be strict enforcement of all federal laws."

Tully shook his head. "Angie, it sounds as if you're about to pull the rug out from under our whole way of life."

She smiled. "I hope so, Bo. So what do you know about the judges and the cash?"

"In regard to the cash, I've never heard of any loose cash floating around Blight County, with taxes paid on it or not. I don't know where such cash would come from. Generally speaking, our judges don't seem to rule over many cases, a divorce here or there, a car wreck from time to time, nothing that would strain their little gray cells. I just had a confrontation with a judge down in Kindle County, though. Their deputies and some state police cowboys barged into my county and arrested an old friend of mine just because he killed three or four cars."

"Cows?"

"No, cars. Haven't you ever heard of anyone killing cars, Angie?"

"Honestly, Bo, I haven't."

Tully shook his head. "You FBI guys are so limited in your experience, I'm surprised you ever get any-body arrested."

"Enlighten me, Sheriff. How do you kill a car?"

"Well, there are different ways. In this case, a bunch of kids roared their fancy cars into the dirt patch old Ed Stokes thinks of as his front yard and started doing wheelies, scaring Ed's free-range chickens half to death, if not killing some of them outright. Ed watched them for a bit from the rocking chair on his front porch, then pulled out his .44 Magnum pistol and blew a hole through the engine block of each car and killed it dead. The kids stopped laughing, jumped out, and ran screaming into the woods. They're from Kindle County, where only the rich folks live, and when they got home they told their parents Ed had tried to kill them. That's when the parents got the state police and Kindle deputies involved."

"So what happened to old Ed?"

"Once I told the judge what had happened, he turned old Ed over to me. Ed's downstairs in jail as we speak."

"So you saved him from jail down in Kindle and put him in jail here."

"Well, he's free to wander around my jail. I keep his cell door open so he can get out and talk to the other prisoners as much as he wants, which isn't too much, I imagine, because they're a pretty stupid bunch. I don't think Ed can stomach their idiocy for too long, so it's good punishment for him. A criminal needs to pay for his crimes. Which reminds me, I told Ed I would go out to his place and feed his chickens. You want to go along for the ride? It will be good for your education of Blight County."

"I think I'm probably educated enough on Blight County, but I wouldn't mind seeing Ed's place. Let's go. His chickens must be getting pretty hungry."

Chapter 28

Driving Angie out to Ed Stokes's place in his Explorer, Tully explained Ed to her. "He's the perfect poor citizen as far as Republicans are concerned."

Angie smiled. "I hope this isn't going to be a political diatribe."

"Not at all. I'm neither Republican nor Democrat, nor a conservative nor a liberal. I feel free to shift my political preference to whichever way the wind is blowing. You might think of me, Angie, as a sailor adrift on a raft in the drifting tides of politics."

Tully braked to let a cow moose and her calf cross the road ahead of them.

Angie smiled. "Yes, well, I've always thought of you as a person adrift."

"Indeed, and my principle is never to run aground on the shore of the losing party."

"It's good to know you have a principle, Bo."

"Thank you. It's a rather rare quality here in Blight County. But I was about to tell you why old Ed Stokes is the perfect citizen for the Republicans."

"Okay, tell me."

Tully cleared his throat. "First of all, he doesn't take one penny from the government."

"Not even Social Security?"

"He's never worked at a job, so I doubt he gets any Social Security. He does make a little money gathering wild mushrooms, huckleberries, and wild honey and selling them to restaurants in town, but I doubt he pays any tax on the money he gets. Other than that, he grows all his own vegetables and fruit and gets his firewood out of downed trees on his place. He did inherit a little farm from his parents. Abe Sutton grows wheat on the farm and shares half the crop with Ed, who feeds his share of the wheat to his chickens. Ed gets his protein from the eggs his chickens lay."

"And he has no other source of money?"

"None I know of. He did fight in the Korean War and got wounded. Maybe he gets some benefit from surviving that, but I don't know. I guess if he gets sick, maybe there's some veterans' benefit he's entitled to, but I've never known him to get sick."

Tully turned off on the dirt road leading through the woods to Ed's place. He pointed out the tidy little shack with Ed's empty rocking chair on the front porch. "Ed was sitting there rocking and keeping an eye out for the coyote that's been raiding his chickens when those kids came roaring in and started doing wheelies in his yard. Without bothering to get out of his rocker, he told me, he lifted that big old .44 Magnum pistol off his lap and killed each of the cars, one after another. Ed laid his gun back on his lap and went on rocking." Bo pointed. "You'll notice the puddles of oil where the cars bled out."

"But where are the chickens?"

"I suspect Ed locked them up in the henhouse before he was dragged off to jail. Come on, we'll give them a little recess."

Angie followed him over to the henhouse. Tully unlatched the door and the chickens came cascading out, squawking their fury at being locked up. He walked inside and lifted the hinged cover on a large wooden bin half-filled with wheat. He picked up a bucket and filled it from the bin, then walked out to the patch of dirt and threw handfuls of it around until the bucket was empty. Then he and Angie sat on the porch, Angie rocking in Ed's chair, and watched the chickens feed. Tully went inside, found half a bottle of Ed's whisky, poured a shot for each of them in a glass, and poured in a dipper of creek water from a pail on the counter. Angie was watching the chickens when he came out. He handed her a glass. She stared at it.

"Whiskey," he said. "Ed makes it himself. I've added some creek water to tone it down a bit. You might notice a hint of wild-bee honey in the flavor."

She sipped. "My goodness, Bo! It's delicious!"

"Yes, old Ed is a bit of a craftsman when it comes to making whiskey."

Angie smiled. "I think this is probably the finest illegal whiskey I've ever tasted."

"I thought you might approve. I poured each of us just enough for a taste, because otherwise your head falls off and rolls around on the ground."

"I'm not surprised." She gave him a look. "I suppose it's never occurred to you how we'll get the chickens back in their house when we have to leave."

"No problem."

"Easy for you to say. I somehow get a picture of you and me racing around catching them one by one, stuffing them in sacks and hauling them back to the henhouse."

"That would be much too labor-intensive, Angie. I'm surprised they don't teach you stuff like this at the FBI Academy."

"Yes, it does seem a strange thing to omit chicken wrangling from the FBI curriculum. Maybe once I observe the technique I will report it to the faculty. I have to admit, Bo, this little place does have a certain charm. It's so peaceful. Imagine being self-sufficient here, never having to worry about satisfying nasty bosses or the general public. I can see why you're intrigued by the old gentleman."

Tully thought about this. Then he said, "Actually, I could never live like this."

"Why not?"

"For one reason, I don't have the knowledge or the talent. Even if I could find a wild-bee tree, I wouldn't have a clue how to get the honey out of it without being stung to death. Ed does it as a matter of routine. Have you noticed the silence here, Angie?"

"Yes, I have. It's deafening, isn't it?"

"It is that. That silence would drive me crazy within a couple of days."

Angie rocked, the chair making tiny squeaks. "I suppose one would get used to it after a while."

"I don't think so," Tully said. "That silence would drive me stark-raving mad. As a matter of fact, I'm already starting to feel a little weird. About time for us to put the chickens back in their henhouse."

Angie laughed and stood up. "Yes, I'm very interested to see how we accomplish that."

As she stared out at the chickens, Tully put two fingers in his mouth and made a piercing shriek. The chickens streaked into the henhouse.

Angie's mouth gaped.

"Hawk," Tully said. "Works every time." He turned and looked at her.

"Wet panties," she said. "That's the first time I've ever heard a hawk scream right next to me. Now turn your head, while I find someplace to put them up to dry."

He noticed she had the gun out of her shoulder bag as he turned his head. "I'd appreciate your putting the gun back in your bag, now that you know it was only a hawk screech."

She put away the gun. "You should warn a person before you do something like that."

"They don't teach you hawk screeches at the FBI Academy?"

"I don't know. Maybe it's one of the skills offered at the end of chicken wrangling."

Chapter 29

On the way back to the office, Tully dropped off Angie at her hotel. Daisy frowned at him when he walked in.

He shook his head. "I wish the FBI could figure things out for themselves, without always looking at me to solve their crimes."

"I bet," Daisy said. "Anyway, Lurch called and wants you to call him in Mexico. Here's his number."

Tully called the number. The Unit answered on the first ring.

"Yeah, Boss?"

"How did you know it was me, Lurch?"

"Because nobody else in the entire world would call me here."

"Where are you?"

"I'm in one of the guest rooms at Fester's Mexican ranch. The ranch has a new owner, an Australian."

"An Australian! How come an Australian would buy a ranch in Mexico?"

"He said it's because he suspects the ranch is sitting on an ocean of oil. His name is Barnaby O'Conner and he already owns a cattle ranch in Australia. He's only been over here a month and already speaks English as good as I do."

"Wow. In only a month. So what's the word on Mrs. Fester?"

"Well, according to Barnaby, she and Jeff got married here on the ranch and then took off on a flight to Australia. They're going to spend some time on Barnaby's ranch."

"See if you can find out their flight number, when it left, and where and when it lands."

"I will, Boss. Maybe Barnaby knows. He set up the whole wedding for them and invited all the folks in the village near here. It was quite a shindig."

"I bet. Oh, I nearly forgot a minor detail, Lurch. Did you check the tread on Hillory's pickup?"

"Yeah, I did. The pickup is still here and I got a match. I took off the tire with the tread that matches our mold, put it in the bed of the pickup, like you told me, and replaced it with the spare. Barnaby said it was okay with him if I took the truck."

"Good. We need that truck and tire, Lurch. They're essential to our case against Mrs. Fester and probably Sheridan. They place Hillory at the scene of the crime and probably Jeff, too. Do you have a department credit card with you?"

"Yeah."

"Well, like we discussed, as soon as you get to Nogales, get yourselves a modest motel for the night and head out for Blight City early in the morning. Drop the rental off where you got it in Tucson, and you and Pap drive the Fester pickup back to Blight."

"Got it, Boss. We'll be home in a couple of days."

"No hurry, Lurch. How's Pap doing?"

"Oh, he's been having a great time, out all night savoring the local cantinas and their señoritas. I'm sure he'll love staying over another night in Nogales."

"I'm sure he will. Give you both a chance to get some of the real flavor of Mexico. Find a first-class restaurant and order some good meals on the department, particularly if you happen to meet some pretty señoritas. You two deserve it."

"You feeling all right, Boss?"

"Yeah, I am. Once you're done entertaining yourselves, get your butts back to Blight City as fast as you can, even if you have to drive day and night."

"Whew! Now you're starting to sound like the boss I know. Well, at least Pap and I get one more night for a wild fling in a great Mexican town."

"That's okay. Just make sure you get a motel on the poorer side of town. The department isn't paying for some extravagant Mexican hotel just so you and Pap can put on a show of being high rollers for the local female population."

Chapter 30

"Angie!" cried Lester Cline, the headwaiter at Crabbs. "I heard you were back in town. Some of the other agents have been eating here, too."

Angie smiled. "I know, Lester. I recommend Crabbs to all of them as the best restaurant in all of Idaho."

"We appreciate the recommendation very much. Let me show you to the table I keep reserved exclusively for you and Bo."

And forty other people who actually tip, Tully thought.

As usual, they both chose the luncheon special, the steak salad. Tully added a bottle of the white zinfandel. After Lester left with their order, Tully said, "So how's your case going with our corrupt lawyers and judges?"

"Not too badly. So far we've tied secret bank accounts to one lawyer. A fairly large portion of the cash was withdrawn about the same time Judge McCrackin made a major judgment in favor of the lawyer's client. What do you think, Bo?"

"Sounds about right."

"It appears McCrackin has found a number of cases in favor of that lawyer, despite the fact that the lawyer appears to be an idiot."

"An idiot? How's that?"

"He bought two very expensive cars for himself and his wife, not to mention he sold his small ranch and bought a house in the million-dollar range. He throws money around like confetti at local nightclubs and keeps women on the side in luxurious pads. Judge McCrackin isn't doing that badly, either."

Tully munched a forkful of salad while he thought about this. "You happen to know of any openings in the Blight County law business?"

"Not right at the moment, but I suspect there may be some soon. It seems as if Blight County is moving into the big time, at least as far as crime is concerned."

Tully munched another forkful of salad. "Well, at last a sign of progress. Up to now I've had to deal only with stuff like stolen chain saws, that sort of thing. I want you to know I come down pretty hard on anyone engaged in chain saw theft."

Angie smiled. "Yes, I know. How about crooked lawyers?"

Tully thought about this. "I guess I'd have to empty out the cells of all our deserving criminals and fill them back up with lawyers. You plan on making any busts soon?"

"Yeah, but we'll probably ship them to Boise, at least for starters."

Chapter 31

When Tully got back to the office, his father was sitting in the briefing room talking to Daisy. "Pap! What are you doing here?"

The old man stood up. He was still lean as a post, six feet tall, and with his Stetson hat pulled low over his eyes, as sinister as ever. Tully didn't even want to think about the number of men Pap had killed when he was sheriff. Nor the number of payoffs he accepted to turn loose guilty parties, particularly the owners of gambling establishments. He still kept in touch with broad sections of the underworld. "Come on in my office, Pap. Daisy has work to do."

She said, "Daisy was enjoying your father's intelligent conversation. It's not often I hear intelligent conversation around here."

Pap laughed and followed Tully into his office, pulled out a chair, and sat down. "The old place hasn't changed much since I was sheriff."

"A little less blood splatter on the walls," Tully said. "So you're back in town flirting with my secretary."

"I can't help myself," Pap said. "I just love all the pretty women."

Tully smiled. "I appreciate your helping Lurch down in Mexico."

"Well, we had a little problem with that, Bo. You got any leads on who did Morg in?"

"Only what you and Lurch came up with. They got married on the ranch down there. Now they're headed for Australia on their honeymoon, if they're not already there."

Pap shook his head. "I'd hate for you to arrest them for the Fester murder, Bo."

"Well, it was the evidence you and Lurch turned up, the tire that matched the tread at the crime scene. That's what makes them our prime suspects. The fact they got married shortly afterward makes a great motive. Your tracking skills put them at the scene and time of the murder. Now that we've got the tire back here, the case will be pretty well closed. Where is the tire, by the way?"

"That's what I come up here to tell you," Pap said. "While Lurch and me was partying in Nogales, somebody stole the tire from the bed of the pickup."

Tully sat for a long while without speaking.

Finally, Pap said, "I don't know what to tell you, Bo. It just never occurred to me anyone would steal an old used tire out of the bed of a pickup. But it was your idea we put it there."

Tully leaned back in his chair and cracked his knuckles. "True, it was my idea."

"I thought it was pretty dumb at the time but didn't want to say anything."

"Yeah, you would think I'd have known better."

"Oh, you knew what you was doin', Bo," his father said. "But don't get too upset about it. It's something I would have done myself, if I'd thought of it. I expect it's just the Blight Way, dumb stuff like that."

Tully nodded. "I suppose it is. Hard to imagine a soft-hearted fellow like Fester shooting eagles, though. So you think maybe his wife killed him, because she knew he was doing just that? Maybe he even tormented her by bragging about it? She was a great lover of wildlife, especially birds, I hear."

"Yeah," Pap said, "I think either Hillory or Jeff Sheridan, her new husband, did him in. But there are other suspects out there. He fooled around with a lot of women, and it's possible one of their husbands or boyfriends got upset with him."

Tully thought about this. "But there's a really weird side to this case, Pap."

"I thought the whole thing was weird."

"How about this, then? The fletching on the arrow that killed Fester was made of eagle feathers."

"Eagle feathers! It's illegal even to possess one eagle feather."

"Yeah. Killing people with them is a bad one, too."

Pap scratched his chin. "Depends on the person. I'd rather kill a person than an eagle."

Daisy stuck her head in the door. "Boss, this came in the mail today. I thought it might be of interest to both you and Pap. It's from Ed's Archery." She handed him an envelope. She had already sliced it open and probably read the contents.

"Great!" Tully said. "Maybe we'll at least get some leads."

He pulled out a note and read it aloud, with Daisy standing in his office doorway.

"Dear Sheriff Tully, as I mentioned to you when you stopped by Ed's Archery the other day, we don't keep track of what our customers buy, but we do keep a list of their names and addresses, so we can send them news of different promotions and sales we may have. If we were to go through thousands of copies of sales receipts, we could probably come up with what each person bought, but it would be enormously time-consuming, unless you have a person on your staff who could handle that chore." He glanced up at Daisy.

She shook her head. "This person isn't handling that chore!"

Tully read down through the list. "Well, this is interesting. Mrs. Morgan Fester was a customer of Ed's Archery. I think that's where she bought that green target I saw hanging on the side of a Fester barn. Here are more names of Ed's Archery customers who live in Blight County—Ben Higgens, Mrs. Wallace Smith, Herbert Cathcart, Wade Gossage, and Jason Jones. Any of those ring a bell, Pap?"

"Only one of any interest—Wade Gossage. He's a pretty heavy dude. Done some time back when I was sheriff, but I don't recollect what for. Maybe it was murder or something else of little consequence."

Tully shook his head. "Yeah, as I recall, murder was a misdemeanor back then."

"I have to admit, we didn't get too worked up about it. But here's something may be of interest to you, Bo."

"And that is?"

"Wade had a very pretty wife. She got to fooling around with some guy and Wade beat her up. So she up and divorced him, took most of his money, what there was of it. Knowing what was good for her, she took off for somewhere. Disappeared, anyway. Maybe Wade had something to do with that."

"You happen to know the fellow she was fooling around with?"

Pap scratched his head. "It's been a while, Bo, since I hung out with that crowd. But I'll tell you who might know."

"And that is?"

"A big biker by the name of Mitch Morgan."

"I know Mitch!"

"Well, he heads up the biggest motorcycle gang in town—actually, the only motorcycle gang in town. He's not someone you want to mess with, Bo."

Tully laughed. "You're right. Mitch knows just about everything that goes on at Slade's and elsewhere in the underworld, too, I imagine. I suspect his gang is responsible for half the crime in Blight County."

Pap said, "I don't think 'half' does the gang justice. Anyway, Mitch might know something about what happened to Wade and, more important, Wade's wife."

Tully nodded. "Good idea, Pap. I'll stop by Slade's and see if I can find that pesky biker. I doubt he'll tell me anything, though."

"You can be awfully persuasive, Bo."

"Pap, you know I would never treat anyone harshly." He went on reading out loud from the Ed's Archery note. "I'm sending you a list of only persons who live in Blight County and who have purchased products over the past year. Best of luck with your investigation, Sheriff. Sincerely, Ed Simpson, Manager and Owner, Ed's Archery."

After work that evening, Tully pulled up and parked half a block from Slade's Bar. He would have parked closer but motorcycles took up all the parking space. He got out and lumbered down the sidewalk, absentmindedly feeling for the blackjack in his hip pocket. There was also a .45 semiautomatic pistol in the shoulder holster under his jacket. In other words, he was properly attired for an evening at Slade's.

Even though it was still early, Slade's was booming, loud laughter oozing out onto the street, harsh language roaring above it, a typical evening at Slade's. Two motorcycles were parked up on the sidewalk, blocking his way. Tully raised a booted foot and sent them crashing out of his way. The noise instantly quieted the ruckus inside. A handful of occupants looked out the open door. Tully shouldered his way through. As usual when he put in an appearance at Slade's, the tavern suddenly went silent and then, bit by bit, began to pick up volume. He looked around the room and found Mitch seated at the bar. The big biker calmly watched him approach and then turned and said something to a fellow seated on a stool next to him. The fellow shook his head. Mitch leaned closer and whispered something to him again. The man quickly evacuated the stool, which Tully then occupied. At least the fellow had warmed it for him.

"What brings you slumming, Bo?" Mitch said. "We don't even have a decent knife fight going on."

Tully smiled. "Just here on routine business, Mitch." The bartender came over, removed the empty glass, and set a full glass of beer in front of him. "Your regular, Bo," he said. "On the house."

"Thanks, Pete." Then he turned his attention to the biker. "I need some help, Mitch, on a murder investigation I'm working on."

Mitch took an uneasy glance around the room, which was slowly rising to its normal volume. "I'll do what I can."

"Do you recall ever knowing a fellow by the name of Wade Gossage?"

Mitch ran his tongue thoughtfully over his teeth, then glanced over his shoulder, apparently to make sure he wasn't in danger of being overheard. "Yeah, I know Wade."

"Is he still around?"

"I'm not sure. He lived for a while with a woman who hung out down here from time to time. I figure she's the one you're curious about. Seems to me they got married at some point. In fact, I think they had been married before and broke up for some reason. Your man Fester zeroed in on her for a while. Gave her clothes and jewels and money, and then they went off somewhere on a trip together. It was just as if Wade didn't exist anymore."

"What happened to her?"

"Nothing much, as far as I know. After Fester got took out of the picture, she moved back in with Wade. He's kind of an ornery cuss, but I think they get along all right now."

"Any idea where they live?"

"Oh yeah, they got themselves a little cabin up on Rattle Creek. Wade does some cruising for the Forest Service and during summers mans a lookout tower. I imagine now he takes his wife along with him to the tower. She's a pretty thing and Wade is smart to take her with him. She gets paid for the lookout duty, too. I, for one, wouldn't leave her on her own. Ole Wade's probably learned his lesson. You think he might have done Fester, Bo?"

"It's possible. I don't have any other leads, at least none I'm happy about."

Mitch slid off his stool. "Well, I don't want to get Wade in trouble, but you might take a look at him. Years ago, I understand he did some guy and served time for it. Generally, though, he seems peaceable enough, not the kind of guy who runs around killing folks for no reason."

Tully said, "I think I know the cabin on Rattle Creek you're talking about. Years ago I used to fish the creek quite a bit."

"Just watch yourself, Bo. I really don't know what kind of state Wade's in these days."

"Thanks, Mitch. I'll keep that in mind."

Chapter 32

Early the next morning, Tully called Daisy from home and told her he was going to pay Wade Gossage a visit on the way into the office.

"Never heard of him," Daisy said. "This related to the Fester murder?"

"Maybe. Seems like something I should check out, though."

The Rattle Creek Road was mostly dirt. The snow had melted off it. Come spring, the road would be up to one's knees in mud, but there was enough frost in the ground now to keep it solid. Rattle Creek was the sort of area that required a certain kind of resident, mostly people at the end of their rope who had started out at the short end to begin with. The creek had risen a little in the warmer days and was now rattling along in justification of its name. Tully spotted the little white house from half a mile away. It sat on a slight rise of ground that would protect it from the occasional spring flooding. As far as Tully could remember, the house was the last one on the creek, before the road began to climb into the mountains. There was a pickup truck in the driveway. Tully pulled in behind it, shut off the engine, and got out. There was a light on in what he thought was probably the kitchen. He didn't know how he might be greeted and reached under his jacket and slid the safety off the .45. He knocked on the door, which was opened by an attractive woman of middle age. He said, "Ma'am, I'm Blight County Sheriff Bo Tully. I don't think we've ever met."

She smiled. "Oh, yes we have, Sheriff. It was years ago. You weren't sheriff then, but I think your father was. You were fishing the crick and stopped by and asked if I might give you a drink of water. I did and we talked a long while. You were still in college, I believe."

"Mrs. Gossage, you have an excellent memory. I loved fishing Rattle Crick. It used to have a nice run of cutthroat trout in June each year. That month was like Christmas to me."

She laughed. "We were all so young then. No offense, Sheriff."

He grinned at her. "None taken. Is your husband in, Mrs. Gossage? I would like to speak to him."

She turned and yelled, "Wade, Sheriff Bo Tully is here to see you!"

A tall, muscular man came lumbering out of a back room, running his fingers through his long graying hair. "What on earth have I gone and done now, Sheriff?"

"Nothing at all that I know of, Mr. Gossage. I've been working on a criminal investigation and someone suggested to me that you might know something about it. The crime has some rather gory aspects to it, and I would just as soon not subject Mrs. Gossage to it. So would you mind if we stepped outside?"

"No problem, Sheriff. Wait till I grab a jacket."

He walked back down a darkened hallway. Tully hoped he would return with only a jacket. He did. They went outside.

Rattle Creek was still rattling away. Tully said, "I love that music."

Gossage looked around. "What music is that, Sheriff?"

"The crick. I used to fish it when I was a kid, the happiest time of my life."

The man stared at the water. "After fifty years of listening to it, I guess I don't hear it anymore. Actually, without this little device, I don't hear much of anything." He tapped the device in his ear.

Tully nodded. "Yeah, I probably could use one of those myself."

"I expect you're here about the Fester murder," Gossage said.

"Yes, I am, Mr. Gossage. I don't have much to go on, and I'm tracking down every tiny lead that comes my way."

Gossage jammed his big hands in his jacket pockets and stared out at the creek. "Well, Sheriff, I make a pretty good suspect. Years ago I would have killed him in the blink of an eye, and even thought quite a bit about doing it. I got in a bit of trouble as a young man, even did some fairly serious time, but as I got older the urge to kill somebody or even something faded away. I gave up hunting years ago and haven't touched a gun in ages. I do love shooting, though, and took up target shooting quite some time ago."

"Must be with a bow and arrow."

"Yep. I read in the *Silver Tip Miner* that Fester was done in the back by an arrow. There was a time I might have shot him myself, but I wouldn't have bothered with an arrow. That seems like a pretty creepy way to kill a person, if you ask me. And he was shot in the back! I would've wanted him to see it coming, to know why he was being killed. He might just as well die of a heart attack, with no idea he was being whacked for fooling around with some other guy's wife."

"Good point, Mr. Gossage. I've wondered about that myself."

"You probably know this already, Sheriff, but Fester made a lot of enemies down at Slade's Bar, fooling with the women there. He had all kinds of money to throw around, and some of the ladies couldn't resist the jewels and flowers and travel and I don't know what all. If I was going to look for his killer, I'd look at Slade's. Come to think of it, if I was you, Sheriff, I wouldn't even bother looking for his killer."

"As a matter of fact, I'm thinking of throwing in the towel as far as this job is concerned, and doing so pretty soon, whether the Fester murder is solved or not."

"Can't blame you for that. Good luck, Sheriff." Gossage walked back to his house, and Tully got in his Explorer and drove back to town.

Chapter 33

When Tully got back to the office, Lurch was standing next to Daisy's desk. Both of them looked uneasy.

"Lurch!" Tully said. "You made it back! Excellent! Come on in the office and tell me all about it."

Lurch gave Daisy an uneasy glance. She gave him a glance back, equally uneasy. He figured they had been talking about his little adventure in Mexico. The deputy followed him into the office, and Tully shut the door behind them.

"So, Lurch, I take it your trip was a success."

"Not exactly, Boss."

"How's that?"

"Well, while we were spending the night in Nogales, somebody stole Mrs. Fester's tire out of the back of the pickup. Yeah, I know, I should have taken it into the motel room with me. It just never occurred to me someone would steal an old used tire. How many people would even have a pickup the tire fit?"

Tully shook his head. "Lurch, putting the tire in the bed of the pickup was my idea. Pap has already told me what happened. Mrs. Fester and Jeff's wedding down in Mexico even gave us a motive! With Morg's murder, Hillory gets the whole shebang—both ranches and even a new husband! But without that tire, there's no way we can place her at the scene and time of the murder!"

"I know, Boss! I know!"

Tully smiled. "Don't get so upset, Lurch. After all, I'm the one who told you to put the tire in the bed of the truck. Who would even imagine somebody stealing a used tire out of the bed of a truck at night in a quiet old Mexican town? It's not your fault. So don't feel bad about it."

"But this means we don't have any evidence that puts Mrs. Fester at the scene and the time of the murder!"

"Oh yeah, but these things happen."

Lurch, looking greatly relieved, got up and left. Tully wandered out to Daisy's desk.

"Whew!" she said. "I was afraid you might fire Byron."

"Ah, we all make mistakes. So, anything else going on here?"

"Well, yes, we did get a telegram from Australia." She ruffled through some papers on her desk.

"Just tell me what it said."

"Hillory wrote that she and Jeff were cutting their honeymoon short and were flying back to the US to clear themselves in Fester's murder."

Tully thought about this for a moment. "Reply to her telegram and put my name on it. Tell her that she and Jeff should finish their honeymoon. No evidence against them exists in the death of Morg Fester."

"Really, Boss?"

"Really, Daisy."

"That's wonderful!"

"I feel pretty good about it myself. Now I have to go visit Judge Patterson. I need a shot of his best booze to celebrate."

"What are you celebrating?"

Tully smiled. "Daisy, after all these years of working in the sheriff's office, you still don't understand the Blight Way, do you?"

"I guess not."

Tully pulled up in front of the judge's house and strolled up the walk. The flower beds were all bare dirt bordered by receding snow. Mildred had apparently moved all of her plants to the sizable greenhouse in the judge's backyard. Once he had retired, Tully thought he would build a huge greenhouse in his backyard. He rang the doorbell. Mildred answered.

"Why, Bo, what a pleasant surprise! Come in, come in!"

He stepped into the hallway. Mildred stood on her tiptoes and kissed him on the cheek. "My goodness, Bo, it's always so good to see you. I hope you have time to sample some of the judge's expensive new gin with me."

"Mildred, the day will never come when I don't have time for that. How is the old man, anyway?"

"Ornery as ever. But as always, he will be happy to see you. You go plop into your favorite chair in his study while I roust the judge out of his den."

Tully strolled into the judge's study. It was as familiar as his own, including the worn pink easy chair Patterson had apparently reserved for him over the years. He took off his hat, dropped it on the floor, kicked off his boots, and put his stockinged feet up on the matching footstool. This room was one of his most favorite places in the world.

The judge came bustling in followed by Mildred. "Bo! Good to see you again so soon."

Mildred turned and dashed off.

Tully said, "Well, Judge, I'll probably have a lot more time in the future to drop by. I'm retiring as sheriff of Blight County!"

"Retiring! You can't do that, Bo! What will the county do without you?"

"I think it will do fine. I'm recommending Brian Pugh as my replacement. You know Brian, Judge. He'll make an excellent sheriff."

The judge nodded. "Yes, I know Brian and I'm sure he'll do fine. But what terrible thing has happened that makes you want to retire?"

Tully leaned forward in the chair and put his hands on his knees. "Well, it's this way, Judge. I suddenly found myself making distinctions between bad guys who kill good guys and good guys who kill bad guys, if you get my drift."

The judge was quiet for a long moment, his brow furled. Then he nodded slightly and said, "Yes, I know the feeling well."

Mildred came into the room with a tray containing three martinis and a pitcher half-full of them. The judge said, "Just in time with the martinis, Mil. Bo is hanging up his badge."

Mildred almost dropped her tray, causing Tully's heart to miss a beat. She steadied herself. "Bo, I don't know whether to laugh or cry."

"I feel the same way," the judge said. "Bo, I can certainly understand you wanting to get away from the crime scene, but what will you do?"

Mildred handed Tully his martini. He took a sip and smiled at her. She smiled back. They both knew she had raided the judge's secret stash.

The judge said, "I don't blame you for wanting to get away from the gritty business of being sheriff, but don't you think you might miss it?"

"That's something I wanted to run by you, Judge. The truth is, I would miss it. So I've been thinking about opening my own private detective agency. That way I could pick and choose my own crimes to solve, rather than just any that come along. Might even do some work for the FBI. I have some contacts there and went through their training program for sheriffs and police officers. Also, when I was a college student, I took a semester course at Washington State University in arson. The lady who ran it was one of the leading arson experts in the world, and it was fascinating. I thought I might make that my specialty. Maybe I'd travel all over the United States solving arson cases. I might even go back to college for a semester and brush up on some of the chemical aspects of it."

The judge sipped his drink and thought about this for a moment. "You know, Bo, that's not a bad idea, setting up your own private detective agency."

Mildred broke in. "But Bo, I heard you just made a major sale of one of your paintings and now wanted to paint full-time."

"It's this way, Mil. I love painting, but you get tired of doing the same thing day in and day out, so I thought maybe I would mix in a little gumshoeing. Also, I have this lady I've promised to drive up the whole length of Idaho on a sightseeing adventure. I figure I could take along a camera and get a lot of pictures to use in my painting. The lady has given me a lot of warnings over the years that have turned out to be right on the money, so I owe her this trip."

"A lady!" Mildred yelped. "Bo, don't you think that's . . ." She didn't finish her sentence.

The judge laughed. "He's referring to his fortune-teller, Mil. I think you may have consulted Etta Gorsich from time to time yourself."

"Oh my! Etta! My goodness, yes! She's wonderful. But Bo, she must be at least seventy years old."

"Not too old to enjoy the scenery of North Idaho. I'll wait until the spring, though, when the snow is off and the new growth is coming on. I may even show her how to find morel mushrooms out in the woods."

"Etta's usually right on the money when it comes to predicting things," the judge said. He reached over and tapped Tully on the knee. "Now *there's* something I'd like you to show Mil and me, how to find morels! Occasionally, one of our outdoorsy lawyers will make us a gift of a few, trying to bribe me, and for morels, I let him! But I'd like Mil and me to learn how to find our own. Lawyers are simply too stingy."

Tully nodded. "I feel the same way, Judge. I never have enough time myself to go after morels in the brief period they come out, not to mention fall mushrooms like shaggymanes. Anyway, Judge, I'm not exactly sure how an elected official resigns from his job."

The judge frowned as he thought about this. Tully finished off his martini. Mildred raised a questioning eyebrow and held up her pitcher, but he covered the top of his glass with his hand. After a moment the judge said, "We don't often have an elected official resign. In fact, I can't remember a single one. Most of them die in office, but that seems a bit extreme in your case. I think all you have to do is write the board of county commissioners a letter, telling them you are resigning your office on such and such a date and for them to arrange an election for your replacement."

"As I told you, I'm going to recommend Brian for the job. He's the best guy I've got and they're all good."

The judge nodded. "I'd be happy to recommend Pugh."

Mildred asked, "So, Bo, when do you plan to resign?"

"I'm handing in my letter of resignation to the secretary first thing tomorrow. No telling how long it will take them to act on it, but I'll be done with the job as soon as a new sheriff takes over."

Chapter 34

Tully paid particular attention to the *klocking* of his three-thousand-dollar boots as he walked for possibly the last time down the marble-chip floor of the courthouse toward the office. It was a sound he would definitely miss. Each *klock* seemed to echo with authority in the hallway. As usual there was a little group of uniformed gossipers crowded around Daisy's desk.

"Ah," he said. "How convenient to have you all assembled here, because I have an announcement to make."

They turned and stared at him. He had never before made an announcement. "My announcement is this. I have just told Judge Patterson that I am resigning as sheriff."

The group sucked in its collective breath.

He went on. "As soon as I turn in my letter of resignation to the secretary of the board of county commissioners, I will be finished as sheriff of Blight County. No doubt one of you gentlemen gathered here in this hen-and-bull session will be appointed sheriff. I will miss all of you, but I am not sad to be leaving. I plan to settle down in the house on my little farm and grow all my own food, heat and cook with firewood I cut out of my own forest, and paint pictures whenever I feel like it. There's one picture in particular I am looking forward to painting."

"What picture is that, Bo?" a deputy asked.

"The one of Daisy."

Daisy gasped. "Of me, Bo? Why on earth would you paint a picture of me?"

He wrinkled his brow and scratched his chin, as if trying to think of a reason. "Well, I guess because you're beautiful. Oh, and before I clean out my desk, I do have one last request."

Daisy shook her head. "There's always one last request, isn't there, Sheriff?"

"Yes, I suppose it must seem that way. But my very last request is this. Daisy, will you marry me?"

She gasped. Then she threw herself into his arms and covered his face with kisses.

"Can I take this as a yes?" he said.

Late that afternoon, Tully decided he was about to drop dead of hunger and couldn't possibly make it home to fix his own dinner. He checked his watch. Ah, it was just about time for the jail kitchen to start feeding the prisoners. He stepped into the rickety elevator and went rattling down into the courthouse basement. Two burly guards from the jail stood at the door to the kitchen. One of them, Carl Jaspers, greeted him.

"How you doing tonight, Bo?"

"To tell you the truth, Carl, I'm beat. Thought I'd join our prisoners for their nightly meal."

"Good choice. I eat here every chance I get. It's something else. The chef—and that's what she is, a chef, not just one of your plain ordinary cooks—is a genius when it comes to food. She's transformed the simple fare of a county jail kitchen into a culinary triumph. Her name is Erin McManus. She's been chef in some of the best restaurants in the Pacific Northwest, and here she is now, feeding the dregs of society. Seems a waste of her talents, to throw them away on a bunch of criminals."

Tully looked around the room. It was full of smiling, expectant faces. He guessed even criminals needed something to look forward to, even if only their meals. His gaze suddenly stopped on one particular diner. He straightened and strode menacingly toward the person, a pudgy man happily lifting a laden fork toward his mouth. It was August Finn, the editor and reporter from the *Silver Tip Miner.*

"Augie! What the devil are you doing here, dining at the county's expense?"

Startled, Augie peered up at him. "What do you mean, Bo, 'the county's expense'? Erin charges me ten dollars for dinner and five dollars each for breakfast and lunch!"

"What! You eat three meals a day here, Augie?"

"Of course not. Only as often as I can manage it. The county jail is the best place to eat in all of Blight

City, maybe in all of Idaho. As a matter of fact, I'm going to write a feature on it."

Tully pulled out a chair and sat down next to the reporter. A car thief Tully had arrested several months before came up and stood over them, a pad in his hand. He removed a pencil from behind his ear. "What would you like, Sheriff?"

"Well, Barney, what are my choices?"

"Coffee, tea, or milk. Otherwise you get the specialty."

"And that is?"

"What Augie is eating."

"In that case I'll take the dinner special with coffee."

"That will be ten dollars, Sheriff."

"You charge everybody ten dollars, Barney?"

"Nope, Sheriff. Us criminals eat for free. Only you and Augie and any stray citizen who wanders in has to pay." He pointed to a group of tan-dressed men sitting at a far table. "Even Fish and Game. They furnish the café with most of its protein."

"Not roadkill, I hope."

"Naw, never roadkill. They get all of their game from poachers and turn it in to the jail, along with the poachers. Several of the criminals here tonight are eating meat they poached themselves."

The reporter had his pad out and was scribbling furiously in it. Tully shook his head in dismay.

"Augie, if you run a feature in the *Silver Tip Miner* that my jail is the best place in all of Idaho to eat, we'll be overrun with people wanting to eat here."

"But they'll all have to pay, Bo. That will help the county finance the jail."

Tully stared at the reporter. "You think the average citizen of Blight County will want to eat with criminals?"

"Why not? Most of them already eat at home with criminals."

"You have a point. Don't quote me, Augie, but this is the best meal I've had in ages. I notice the chef manages to get the perfect flavor of venison in the meat."

"Yeah, and here's another whole mystery for you, Bo. Sometimes she even manages the flavor of elk or moose."

Tully dug in his pants pocket, dragged out a rumpled ten-dollar bill, and handed it to the waiter. He watched Barney walk back toward the cashier and hand him something, probably an old parking ticket, if he knew Barney as well as he was sure he did.

That evening, driving down to his house, he glanced up at his woods. The trees were packed with eagles, their white topknots glowing like Christmas tree ornaments. He smiled and said, "Well, ladies and gentlemen, you will be safe here from now on. I catch anyone shooting at you, you can feast on his dead carcass for breakfast the next morning." He glanced out to the middle of his lower hayfield, and there, glowing in the middle of it, was a large, perfect circle drawn in the freshly fallen snow. No footprints led to or away from it. His foot hit the brake and the Explorer skidded to a stop on the icy road. Now, at last, the mystery would be solved. He pulled on the hand brake, got out, and started wading through the snow down to the circle. When he came to it, he stepped carefully over the perfect line of the circumference, cut about an inch deep into the snow. He guessed the circle was more than six feet across. Then he waded over to the hole in the middle, where the point of the protractor must have stuck. He shined his flashlight into the hole. At the bottom of it he could see the imprints of an eagle's claws, where they had pivoted tightly around. Now he knew an eagle had flown in there, spread its wings out to full length so that the tip of each just touched the snow. Then it had turned in a full circle. After completing its task, it flew off, leaving no tracks leading to or away from the circle.

Tully turned and looked back at the eagles roosting in the woods and said to them, "You're welcome, ladies and gentleman! I don't know what your message says, but I appreciate it anyway!"

Then he walked back to his Explorer, got in, and started driving the rest of the way down to his house. He smiled. There was a light on in his living room.

THE SILVER TIP MINER

January 4, 2013
Blight County Sheriff Bo Tully Retires
By
August Finn

Eight years ago, I graduated with a degree in journalism from a university in the eastern United States whose name is so precious I will not venture to mention it here in Idaho, and particularly not in the *Silver Tip Miner*. It was Bo Tully himself who advised me to keep my eastern origins a secret. There is no opinion I respect more than that of Sheriff Tully, and so I have striven over the years to keep my origins unknown to the general public of Blight County. Indeed, the sheriff has tried to keep some of his own origins unknown to me and also the fact that he is extremely well educated. I will strive to disclose all of that, as well as point out some of his accomplishments while in office.

Although Sheriff Tully had never taken a course in journalism—in fact, he did not even know such a thing existed—it was he who taught me journalism's true basics, principles apparently unknown to any of my former professors. Such is the sorry state of higher education today, especially in Ivy League schools, whose professors chose to keep such principles secret from me, if they even knew of them. And so it is that now, on the sad occasion of Sheriff Tully's quitting public office, I will attempt to set forth a few of his great accomplishments as the top law enforcement officer of Blight County, Idaho.

No holder of public office in the history of Blight County, with the exception of Sheriff Tully, has ever voluntarily chosen to remove himself from an abundant living provided by the taxpayers of the county. To have done so would have been regarded by Blight residents as evidence of insanity and reason enough for that person to have been otherwise removed. There is evidence of some commissioners still drawing their monthly salary after having been dead for several years. But Sheriff Tully is not dependent on the taxpayers of Blight County. Not only is he modestly wealthy, but I have come upon secret information that one of his latest watercolor paintings sold for an astonishing twelve thousand dollars! My informants tell me that he will now retire to his little farm, grow his own fruits and vegetables, hunt and fish, and cut his own firewood out of his own private forest. I realize that seems a grim kind of retirement to most of us, but here in Blight County we always say, "To each his own." I don't know what that means, but it is what we always say.

I here present a brief history of Sheriff Tully's major accomplishments:

Some years ago the meager remains of a miner were discovered in a small, collapsed mine on Deadman Creek in northern Blight County. Sheriff Tully determined that the remains belonged to a miner who had been murdered near the end of the nineteenth century, approximately the time of the Spanish-American War. He set out to solve the murder and did. Although the murderer was now long dead of old age, Tully managed to identify him as the culprit and even tracked down the murder weapon at a local museum. The complexity of the crime was staggering. Even so, Tully managed to solve it, leaving time itself to bring the criminal to justice.

Last year, three young men were shot to death in a huckleberry patch far back in the mountains. Although no one could understand why anyone would be killed for picking huckleberries, Tully once again solved the murders and brought the culprits to justice. The difficulty of solving this crime cannot be exaggerated, but Tully somehow managed to do it, with the assistance of beautiful FBI agent Angie Phelps. I have a note from Agent Phelps telling me that her efforts to establish chicken wrangling at the FBI Academy have proved fruitless. She also informs me that there seems to be little chance of the Bureau's adopting the Blight Way.

One of Tully's most difficult cases was the murder of a young former bank teller shot by a sniper on Chimney Rock Mountain while fleeing a bank robbery. The teller's body was colored a bright yellow by falling tamarack needles, which offered not the slightest clue to the solution of the case but provided a rather pleasant tint to the whole mystery.

An avalanche made the solution of another case particularly difficult, but once again Sheriff Tully managed to overcome all obstacles, including a great deal of snow. Casts made of footprints in the snow became major clues in this mystery, as well as a description of just how such casts are made. The average reader may find such information boring, but there exist mystery buffs who will peruse it with keen interest, looking for errors.

Many of Tully's cases involved the peculiar concept known as the Blight Way. I keep encountering it as I report on Sheriff Tully's efforts to bring law and order to Blight County, but after several years of closely following his various methods devoted to law enforcement, I am as confused about it as ever.

I will now give a brief biography of Sheriff Tully. He was born in 1965 and grew up in the lap of luxury, a rare occurrence for citizens of Blight. The reason for the luxury was simply that a certain amount of wealth was passed down to him from his father, his grandfather, and his great-grandfather, all of whom were sheriffs of Blight County. Prior to Bo, Tully sheriffs apparently held the record for most corrupt in the whole history of the state. Some of this wealth was passed on to Bo, who used a portion of it to enroll in the University of Idaho as an art major. His mother, Katherine Rose McCarthy— or, to be more complete, Katherine Rose McCarthy Tully O'Hare Tully Casey—was the sole source of stability over the course of Bo's childhood.

I have derived from an extremely reliable source the reason Bo has given for resigning as sheriff of Blight County. The source told me that Bo had explained to him that he had started distinguishing between bad people who kill good people and good people who kill bad people. The law, of course, requires that they all be treated the same, according to their guilt or innocence. This brings us back to the Blight Way. It is a mysterious concept that allows, as far as I can make out, a certain degree of elasticity in the execution of legal matters.

But Bo Tully is not vanishing from Blight County public life. I am informed by a reliable source that he will soon open the Bo Tully Private Detective Agency and thereby go on solving assorted crimes without the *Silver Tip Miner* peering over his shoulder. Well, good luck with that, Bo.

I have just received a letter from Sasha McBride, the former chef at Silver Tip, our local hotel for professional ladies. Sasha reports that she is working hard on her doctorate in ornithology, specializing in eagles. She says she has just made an amazing discovery, which is that it appears there is a causal relationship between eagles and circles in the snow. She reports that she has discovered that circles in the snow are a worldwide phenomenon, but only in areas that receive snow and are visited by eagles. Sasha has explained the circles as an expression of the eagles' gratitude for some action they interpret as a favor done for them by humans. Since the circle that occurred in the Silver Tip area was in close proximity to the murder site of Morgan Fester, an alleged suspect in the shooting of eagles, Sasha is of the opinion that Fester's murder resulted in a circle in the snow, an expression of gratitude for that service from our visiting eagles. I will reserve my own opinion about this theory, except to say that

Bo Tully may be right in his opinion about the state of modern higher education.

Erin McManus and the Blight County Jail Kitchen

What is the very best place to eat in all of Blight City? Here is a surprise for all of my readers. It is the Blight County jail, where Chef Erin McManus holds forth as the supreme culinary artist of the entire Blight region. Erin has worked as a chef in nearly all of the finest restaurants in the Pacific Northwest. When her car suddenly imploded while driving through Blight City, she found herself without anything to do while her vehicle was undergoing massive repairs. It was then that she heard the Blight County jail was looking for a new head cook. She applied for and got the job. The jail almost instantly became the favorite eating spot of the city's denizens, with meals available to the general public at rates of $5 for breakfast and lunch and $10 for dinner. Suddenly our local citizens found themselves dining beside our local criminals, the criminals eating for free and the public eating for the above-mentioned charges. Much of the meat for the restaurant comes from local poachers arrested for the crime, several of whom are currently enjoying meals prepared from game animals they themselves poached. The money paid by the dining public goes to finance the jail kitchen. The new jail chef has provided me with a list of dishes she is offering to diners over the following week, along with snacks. Here they are:

DINNER

Monday: Grouse gravy with biscuits

Tuesday: Fried cutthroat trout and toast with a side dish of huckleberries

Wednesday: Corned moose and baked potatoes

Thursday: Elk burgers and fries, wild-berry cobbler

Friday: Largemouth bass and chips

Saturday: Antelope spaghetti with walnut pesto, garlic bread, and homemade ice cream with huckleberry sauce

LUNCH and SNACKS

Elk jerky
Deep-fried frog legs
Pheasant liver pâté
Creole sauce and crawfish
Deep-fried whole wild morel mushrooms
Black bear tartare and toast points
Moonshiner fry bread

BREAKFAST

Monday: Elk sausages and waffles

Tuesday: Huckleberry pancakes and bacon

Wednesday: Country scrambled eggs with wild mushrooms

Thursday: Fried deer liver and French toast

Friday: Fried wild trout and fresh-baked biscuits

Saturday: Fried mystery meat (supplied by Old Gabe Hawkins, who is serving thirty days)

Bo Tully to Wed

Bo Tully and his secretary of many years, Ms. Daisy Quinn, have announced their engagement to be married the first week of spring. Their honeymoon will consist of a leisurely drive through our beautiful state of Idaho, accompanied by Miss Etta Gorsich, Blight City's most prominent fortune-teller.

Until next issue, I am

August Finn, Editor and Sole Reporter, the *Silver Tip Miner*